I was passing a playground and I looked over and saw this little girl on the swings. Her back was to me, but she had long blond hair and she was wearing a red shirt and a red hairband. I kept watching her and all of a sudden it was like time moved backward and I heard Allison's voice say: "Push me higher, Beth! Higher!"

And I heard myself say, "I'm tired of pushing you. Learn how to pump your legs, Allison. I can't push you forever."

And I kept thinking Allison! Allison! And all of a sudden I yelled, "Allison!"

The girl on the swing stopped and turned. She looked right at me. Then she jumped off the swing and ran away. I don't blame her. She probably thought I was crazy. Maybe I am.

Sometimes I think I see Allison or Doug in a crowd at the mall. But, of course, I don't. It's not real. It's never real.

THE GIRL
DEATH LEFT
BEHIND

Lurlene McDaniel

THE GIRL
DEATH LEFT
BEHIND

BANTAM BOOKS
NEW YORK • TORONTO • LONDON • SYDNEY • AUCKLAND

RL: 5.2, AGES 012 AND UP

THE GIRL DEATH LEFT BEHIND

A Bantam Book/May 1999

ISBN: 0-553-57091-9

Published simultaneously in the United States and Canada

Bantam Books are published by Bantam Books, a division of Bantam
Doubleday Dell Publishing Group, Inc. Its trademark, consisting of
the words "Bantam Books" and the portrayal of a rooster, is
Registered in U.S. Patent and Trademark Office and in other
countries. Marca Registrada. Bantam Books, 1540 Broadway, New
York, New York 10036.

PRINTED IN THE UNITED STATES OF AMERICA

OPM   10 9 8 7 6 5 4

To my beloved father,
James G. Gallagher
(1910–1998)

"Listen, I tell you a mystery: We will not all sleep, but we will all be changed—in a flash, in the twinkling of an eye, at the last trumpet. . . . Where, O death, is your victory? Where, O death, is your sting?"

I CORINTHIANS 15: 51–55
(NEW INTERNATIONAL VERSION)

SUMMER

1

"You know the worst thing about my family?" Beth Haxton didn't wait for an answer from her friend and next-door neighbor, Teddy Carpenter. "They're always in my face. I never have any privacy at home." She released the basketball and watched it sail through the rusty rim anchored to the side of Teddy's garage.

Saturday-morning sunshine warmed her back, and from down the street came the sound of a neighbor's lawn mower. Teddy's radio, tuned to a rock station, sat on the stone ledge that ran the length of the driveway. Beth's family had lived next door to

Teddy's for years on Signal Mountain, over-looking Chattanooga, Tennessee. Their families were tight with each other, their mothers great friends. Beth and Teddy had played together, gone to school together, practically grown up together.

Teddy scooped up the ball and took aim. "Why do you need privacy?"

"You're asking me? Don't you remember all the times you used to complain about your brother?"

"Sure, he was a pain when he lived here, but I sort of miss him now that he's not around." Teddy flashed her a grin. "Plus there's no one to blame my messes on. Mom automatically knows it's me."

Teddy's older brother, David, had gone off to college in September, leaving Teddy alone with his parents. Now that it was June, David would be coming home for the summer, which meant that Teddy would get a dose of reality very soon. Then maybe he'd be more sympathetic, Beth told herself. She said, "I hate sharing the bathroom with Doug and Allison. She uses my shampoo and other hair stuff without ever asking. And as for Doug"—she rolled her eyes—

"well, seven is a creepy age, let me tell you. He collects bugs and stores them in bottles on the windowsill."

Teddy shot the ball, and it swished through the hoop. "Nothing wrong with keeping bugs. We used to catch a few ourselves."

"Fireflies," Beth said. "And we always let them go."

Teddy dribbled toward the basket, jumped, and dunked it through the hoop effortlessly. "Two points for me!"

"No fair! You're taller."

"Too bad, shrimp." He patted the top of her head.

Beth made a face at him, snatched the ball, and took a run at the basket. They were both fourteen, but Teddy had suddenly shot up, and he towered over Beth. It irked her because until his growth spurt, she'd always had the edge when they shot baskets.

Teddy asked, "What do you hear from Marcie?"

It was no secret that Teddy had a thing for Beth's best friend. "She's coming over this afternoon." Beth slid him a glance in time to watch his Adam's apple wiggle as he swallowed. "I may bring her over to shoot some baskets. If you're nice to me, that is."

"Aren't I always nice to you?"

"It depends on how bad you want to see my friends." She watched his face color. It wasn't nice to tease him, but it was fun. "Oh, stop looking hyper. I'll bring her over."

"Do what you want. I may not even be home."

"Sure," Beth said. "Just like Allison won't be using my stuff anymore."

Teddy dribbled, made a run around Beth, and shot from outside. The ball swished through the hoop. "Do like I did when your family gets on your nerves. Pretend you're an orphan and come out here and shoot baskets. That's how I handled it when I felt picked on." Breathing hard, he stood in front of her and looked down. "How do you think I got so good at this game?"

"And so humble," she fired back.

Teddy laughed. "Want to go again?"

The honk of a horn interrupted them, and Beth turned to see the Haxtons' van pulling into the driveway. "Rain check," she said.

"Allison and Dad are home from soccer practice. Got to run."

"I got two goals in the scrimmage," eleven-year-old Allison told Beth as she climbed out of the van. Her hair was sweaty, and dirt streaked her cheek. She kicked her soccer ball up onto the porch.

"Well, rah, rah," Beth said without enthusiasm.

"You coming to my game next Saturday?"

"We all are," their father interjected. "We like watching you play."

Beth knew it would be useless to argue. Hers was a family that did everything together—Allison's soccer games, Doug's T-ball games, her own middle-school track events. "Support," Paul Haxton, her father, called it. *Boring*, Beth usually thought. The only time it was fun for her was whenever Marcie came to the fields with her family and they flirted with the older guys.

"Wash up," Carol Haxton said as Beth and Allison trekked into the kitchen. "And Allie, take off your cleats. You're making dents in the floor."

"Oops, sorry."

Beth sighed dramatically. Their mother had to tell Allison the same thing after every soccer event. You'd think the girl could remember it by now.

Doug bounded into the kitchen. "I'm hungry."

"Lunch is almost ready."

He headed for the pantry.

"No snacking," their mother called over her shoulder.

"Aw, Mom, I'm starving."

"Why don't you eat some of those bugs you've been saving?" Beth suggested.

Doug stuck out his tongue at her.

"Mom, Doug's acting jerky," Allison said in a singsong voice.

"All of you stop it," Carol Haxton said sharply. "Honestly, can't you get along for a day? Having the three of you in the room together is like having a pack of dogs fighting over a food dish."

Doug scooted out the door. Allison plopped her cleats into the mudroom. "I'm taking a shower."

"Stay out of my shampoo," Beth warned. She turned to their mother. "She uses it all the time, Mom. Why can't she buy her own?"

"Sharing with her occasionally won't ruin your life, you know."

"Sharing? She almost sucks every bottle dry!"

Her mother set a salad bowl on the table. "I'll speak to her. Set the table, please."

"It's Allison's turn."

"Didn't she just go up to shower?"

"She owes me a turn," Beth grumbled.

"I talked to your aunt Camille this morning."

"How's she doing?" Camille was Beth's mother's sister, and she lived in Tampa, Florida, with her husband and her daughter, Terri. Beth's mother was close to her younger sister, and hardly a week went by when the two of them didn't phone one another.

"She's fine. Busy as ever running Terri places. Did you know that your cousin won an essay contest at her school and is headed to Tallahassee to read it in front of the governor at a special luncheon?"

Beth mumbled an appropriate response.

"Actually, Camille and I were discussing an idea, and I'd like to get your thoughts on it."

Beth froze. When her mother used that tone of voice, she expected trouble. "Like what?"

"We talked about the possibility of Terri's coming for a nice long visit this summer. She can stay in your room and sleep on the cot. You can do things with her and all your friends—I think the two of you would have a great time together. Tell me, what do *you* think?"

2

"What did you tell her?" Marcie sat cross-legged on Beth's bed, eyes wide with curiosity. And sympathy.

"I asked if we could talk about it some other time." Beth flopped backward on the bed and stared up at the ceiling. "Geez—can you imagine being stuck with Terri half the summer? It would be a nightmare!"

"Maybe she's changed." Terri's family had come to Beth's over the Christmas holidays when both of them had been twelve. But Terri had acted totally snotty toward Beth's friends, so no one had liked her.

"I doubt it. She's so spoiled rotten that

nobody likes being around her. She doesn't have any friends in Tampa.'' Beth's family had visited with her aunt's this past Christmas, and as far as her hanging out with her cousin was concerned, it had been a disaster. "I'm telling you, Marcie, *Allison* acts more mature than Terri. Terri threw a tantrum at the mall because her mother wouldn't let her buy this way expensive sweater. I was totally embarrassed."

"Didn't her mother do anything?"

"Tried to reason with her. Kept saying, 'But, Terri, honey, you got three new sweaters at Christmas. You don't need another.' " Beth sat up. "Terri whined and carried on until her mother caved."

Marcie shook her head. "My mom would have grounded me for a week if I acted that way in public."

"Mine too. Even Doug knows how to behave in the mall."

"But now you're going to be stuck with her."

"It sure looks like it." Beth sighed. "I like Aunt Camille and Uncle Jack, but Terri is something else."

"Maybe she's so spoiled because she

doesn't have any brothers or sisters. If you don't ever have to share, then you don't learn the concept."

"What am I going to do? Mom and Aunt Camille are sisters *and* best friends. They even had a double wedding!"

"That's sort of romantic sounding. We aren't sisters, but we could do that too."

"Mom will probably insist I wait until Terri gets married first," Beth said glumly. "As if any guy's ever going to ask her."

Beth had heard the story a hundred times about how her mother and Camille had been pregnant together while their husbands were in the army. Of how she'd been born and then "just three weeks later" Terri had been born. "Camille had a beautiful little girl because I had a beautiful little girl," Beth's mother always joked.

Beth had heard how she and Terri had shared a crib, had been pushed in identical strollers, and had taken baths together every night until they both turned two and the army tour of duty ended. Then Terri's dad landed a job in Tampa, and Beth's father got a job in Chattanooga. Every Christmas, one family or the other made the ten-hour drive to visit. But now her mother wanted Terri to spend almost a month with them. How was she going to survive?

The sound of a lawn mower starting up made Beth scoot off the bed and go to her window. She looked down to see Teddy pushing a mower. "Come here, Marcie," Beth said, raising her window.

Together they leaned out and watched Teddy follow the mower across the slope of his backyard. He wore denim shorts, no shirt, and a baseball cap. "Should I whistle?" Marcie asked.

"He's showing off his bod just for you. Are you impressed?" Beth elbowed her friend.

"Not much of a bod. Unless you like scarecrows."

The two girls began to giggle, then were convulsed with laughter. Beth couldn't help thinking that if her cousin had been as much fun to be with as Marcie, having her visit wouldn't have been a problem. But she wasn't. No, indeed, she wasn't.

"Have you given any thought to what I asked you about Terri's visiting?"

Beth and her mother were at the grocery store, in the produce aisle, when her mother asked the question Beth had been dreading.

"You know, Mom, Terri and I don't have a lot in common."

"I realize that the two of you aren't close like Camille and I are, but you're the closest thing to a sister Terri will ever have, you know."

Beth had heard many times that Camille and Jack had been unable to have another baby. "Terri should have a friend in Tampa to be her almost-sister. Like Marcie is to me."

"But you and Terri are blood relatives. That should count for something. And you know what they say," her mom added with a teasing smile. " 'You can pick your friends, but you can't pick your relatives.' "

"That's what you always say about me and Allison." Beth pursed her lips. How could she make her mother understand that she and Terri had nothing in common beyond their bloodlines?

"Listen, honey." Her mother put a hand on Beth's shoulder. "I'm not going to force you to spend a few weeks with Terri this summer. But I'd really appreciate it if you did let her come. I think Jack and Camille need some alone time."

Who wouldn't? Beth thought. Having Terri around constantly would make anybody crazy. "Oh, all right," she told her mother grudgingly. "Invite her."

Her mother squeezed her shoulder. "Thank you, Beth. I appreciate your doing this. I'll call Camille and tell her, but it would be really nice if you'd write Terri a note and invite her. It would make her feel that this was less of a put-up job, if you know what I mean."

Beth nodded. "When should I invite her?"

"How about mid-July through the first week in August? That way you'll still have plenty of time before school starts again. Will Marcie be around?"

"She's going off on vacation the whole month of July," Beth said with dismay. Which meant she would have to entertain Terri on her own.

"You know your dad and I'll plan some activities. How about a day up at Fall Creek Falls?"

"How about Dollywood?" Beth's family hadn't been to that theme park in ages.

"A good possibility."

"And Six Flags in Atlanta?"

"Don't get greedy," her mother said with a laugh.

Beth shrugged. "It was worth a try."

Her mother forged ahead with the shopping cart. Beth felt mollified. If she had to have her cousin hanging around for part of her summer, then at least she'd keep Terri busy. Alone time had to be avoided. That way they wouldn't be able to get on one another's nerves. *The things I don't do for family*, Beth told herself, and trotted off to join her mother in the cereal aisle.

When David got home from college, the Carpenters invited Beth and her family over for a barbecue. David brought along a pretty blond girlfriend named Shelby from Atlanta, and on the evening of the cookout, they sat in a backyard swing, holding hands and talking in low whispers.

"What's it like having your brother home again?" Beth asked Teddy.

"You mean King David?" Teddy looked

disgusted. "He hardly has time for me. We used to shoot baskets together, but now there's Shelby. I guess that's the problem with being the youngest—everyone forgets about you when the oldest comes home. You're lucky, Beth."

"How so?"

"You'll get to leave the others behind because you'll get to move out first."

"How lucky can I be if I have to have Terri stay with me for three weeks?"

"I'll hang with you."

"That would be good." The wind had picked up, and dark clouds had gathered above the trees.

"Your father's company still having the picnic on the fourth?" Teddy asked.

"Just like every year. Want to come?"

"My dad's taking me and some of the guys from the basketball team down to Six Flags for the weekend."

"Sounds like fun." Beth felt a twinge of envy. With Marcie gone and Teddy away, she'd be bored stiff at her father's company's annual picnic. So far her summer wasn't shaping up to be a winner. She actually found herself wishing for school to start.

Suddenly a bolt of lightning split the sky and a clap of thunder shook the very air. Allison shrieked, and their mother yelled, "You kids come inside this minute." The whole bunch of them scrambled as the wind swayed the tree branches overhead. Beth grabbed bowls of food and made it inside just as a torrent of rain swept across the wooden deck. Everyone grumbled or made jokes about barbecues attracting rain the way picnics did ants.

Beth stared out at the pelting, drenching rain and sighed. She hoped it wasn't a bad omen. What a way to start the summer.

3

"You know, Beth, I could let your father take Doug and Allison, and I could stay home with you."

Beth rested her elbows on the kitchen table, watching her mother fill the picnic cooler with bags of fresh fruit and plastic bowls filled with salads. "Mom, I'm fine. I just feel weak, that's all."

"You've had a nasty flu bug and I'm not sure I should go off and leave you alone all day."

"But the picnic—"

"Will happen again next year, just like it always does," her mother finished.

"I've got plenty to amuse me. I've got books to read, the CD player. You don't have to stay with me, Mom. I can handle a day at home by myself." Beth's bout with flu had started two days before. She did feel better, but not up to being out at the lake all day. It would be the first time she'd missed the annual picnic.

Her mother opened the refrigerator door. "There's plenty for you to eat."

"Please don't say the word *eat*."

As her father entered the kitchen, Beth and her mother exchanged glances. "Carol, where's my Vols baseball hat?" he asked.

Her mother straightened. "You're not wearing that shirt, are you?"

"What's wrong with it? It's clean."

The faded old shirt was her father's favorite. A variety of years-old stains dotted the front. Once-orange letters reading TENNESSEE VOLUNTEERS, the name of the team at her father's alma mater, had faded to a pale peach color.

"It looks awful," his wife said. "What will people think?"

Beth's parents had the same discussion every year. "Why don't you wear the one we bought you for Father's Day?'' Beth suggested.

"Yes," her mother said. "It looks so much better. And the kids picked it out themselves."

"But this is my favorite." He grinned. "And it's lucky, too. Whenever I wear it, my team wins."

"Well, maybe it's time to start a new tradition."

"Please, Dad."

"Oh, all right. But if we lose, I'll know why!" He headed out of the kitchen.

Allison chased Doug into the room, yelling, "Give it back, Doug!"

"Make me!" Doug darted under the table, holding his sister's soccer ball.

"Mother!"

"Stop it, you two. I'm not up to a whole day of your bickering."

"He's such a little brat!" Allison scooted under the table and began to scuffle with her brother.

Beth moved her legs, but not before they got hit by Allison's flying fist. "Ouch!"

"That's it." Her mother stamped her foot.

"Both of you, out. Go to your rooms until we're ready to leave."

"Aw, Mom," Doug said. "We were just playing."

Allison clutched her recovered soccer ball to her chest. "Can I stay home with Beth?"

Beth shook her head. The last thing she wanted was to baby-sit her kid sister. "I'm sick, remember? I can't be watching Allison and resting too."

"You're coming with us, Allie," their mother said.

Beth peered out the large bay window overlooking their backyard. Golden morning sunlight beat down on blooming hydrangea bushes, rows of geraniums, morning glories, and tangles of lacy ferns. The yard was their mother's pride and joy. "At least the rain stopped."

"The weatherman says we should have a pretty nice day, but those sudden thunder-showers never fail to hit our picnic." Carol Haxton turned to Beth. "You know we'll be late getting in."

"I know." The fireworks didn't go off until after nine.

"Are we ready?" Beth's father called from the foyer.

"Come get the cooler."

Beth, still in her sleep shirt, shuffled out to the driveway, where the minivan was loaded and ready to go. Her mother glanced up. Overhead, banks of dark clouds had replaced bright blue sky.

"Honey, did you pack the rain gear?" She asked. "I don't trust the weatherman."

Her father placed one hand on Doug's shoulder to stop the boy in midrun and the other on his wife's arm. "It'll blow over. What's a picnic without rain?"

"We'll get soaked."

"There's a covered pavilion."

"That we'll have to share with a hundred other people."

"Aren't women sissies?" he said to his son.

"Yup, sissies," Doug echoed.

Carol gave up the argument and turned to Beth. "Are you sure you'll be all right?"

"Fine."

"Now, remember the rules. Doors locked. Don't tie up the phone. Call Faye next door if you have any problems." Teddy's mother, Faye Carpenter, hadn't gone off to Atlanta.

Beth started feeling queasy again. She would be glad when everyone had left so that she could lie down. She smiled gamely. Her parents hugged her goodbye. "Hit a home run for me," she told her father.

"I'll give it the best I can without my lucky shirt."

Beth watched them pile into the van. Through the windows, she saw Allison burying her face in a book and Doug playing one-handed catch with a baseball. Beth waved as they pulled out of the driveway. Her father waved, and her mother blew her a kiss. At the end of the street, her father gave a farewell honk with the horn. Beth returned to the house, locked the door, and leaned heavily against it.

After the morning chaos, the house seemed eerily quiet. Beth dragged up the stairs. She headed down the hall toward her room, which until only recently she'd shared with Allison. Her mother had turned her sewing room into a bedroom for Allison so that Beth could have her own space. This made Beth happy. She'd been tired of sharing a room with her kid sister.

Beth passed her parents' room. The bed was neatly made, but her father's crumpled favorite shirt lay wadded on the floor. Allison's yellow, white, and lavender room looked tidy, but Doug's was a disaster. Toys spilled over the carpet, and his bed looked as if he'd been jumping on it. In her own bedroom, she snuggled beneath the covers. In minutes her eyelids drooped.

She was startled awake, her heart hammering, when the boom of thunder shook the house. "Great," she muttered. Rain pelted her window and thudded on the roof. She burrowed deeper beneath the sheets and pictured the picnic area out by the lake. People would be scampering for cover and her mother would be grousing because they had brought no rain gear. Beth was glad she had stayed home.

She slept again, and when she awoke, the rainstorm had passed and the afternoon was fading into evening. She felt better and, suddenly, hungry. Sleepily she headed downstairs to the kitchen, where she searched the refrigerator for something that would taste good but not revolt in her stomach.

She decided on a peanut butter and jelly sandwich and was spreading grape jam on bread when the unexpected sound of the doorbell made her jump straight off the floor. She scampered to the front door and peeked through the filmy curtain covering the long foyer window. She saw two uniformed policemen and her father's secretary standing on the front porch. Her mouth went dry. "Is something wrong?" she called through the door.

"Beth, remember me, Jill Bledsoe?"

"Yes."

"Honey, it's all right to open the door. We . . . we need to talk to you."

"About what?"

"There's been an accident, Beth," Jill said in a halting, frightened voice. "Your family's hurt. We're here to drive you to the hospital where they've been taken. Please hurry."

4

Beth fumbled with the lock, jerked open the door, and let her father's secretary and the two policemen into the foyer.

"Oh, honey, I'm so sorry," Jill said.

"What kind of accident? A car accident? Is it bad?" Fear squeezed Beth's heart.

"Yes, a car accident. I kept looking for them to show up at the picnic site and when they didn't, I got worried. I mean, we had a terrible storm come up."

"I heard the thunder." Beth felt sick to her stomach, but not because of the flu.

"Anyway, my husband and I decided to go see if they'd had car trouble or something and about five miles from the lake, on that old winding road, I saw a van, your family's, down in a ditch and—"

One of the officers interrupted Jill. "They've been taken to Memorial Hospital."

"Are they okay? Will you take me to them now?"

"That's why we're here," Jill said.

Beth ran upstairs and dressed quickly. Her hands shook, and she was so cold that her teeth chattered. Her family had to be all right. They had to be!

She was hurrying to the police car when Teddy's mother came running over from next door. "What's going on?"

The officer spoke quietly to Faye Carpenter. She came over and put her arms around Beth. "I'm going to follow you to the hospital in my car," she said. "I won't let you go through this alone."

When the police car arrived at the emergency room, Beth leaped out as soon as the door was opened. People sat in chairs against the walls in the waiting area. She searched the faces but saw no one she knew. By now, Faye and Jill had caught up to her. Beth whirled and looked at Jill. "Where are they? Where's my family?"

"I don't know. Let me see what I can find out."

Jill crossed to the information desk while Faye stayed with Beth. Jill and the woman behind the desk talked; then the woman left. By now the police officers had also joined Beth.

"The receptionist said she has to get the doctor who's handling the case. She said we should stay here and wait," Jill said when she returned to the group.

Minutes later the receptionist came out with a nurse, who introduced herself and said, "Dr. Higdon is the doctor handling your family's case. He'll be out to talk to you as soon as he can get away."

"But I want to see my parents. Where are they? Are they okay?"

The nurse asked, "Dear, is there someone I can call to come be with you?"

Faye said, "I'm with her."

"Are you a family member?"

"Her neighbor. But her mother and I are friends."

"I'd like to have a relative here," the nurse said. "Do you have grandparents? Anyone we can call?"

Beth shook her head. Her grandparents were dead. "My aunt Camille lives in Tampa."

"Do you know her phone number?"

"I—I don't remember." Beth could hardly remember her own name at the moment.

"Just tell me what you can and I'll track her down via the phone company," the receptionist said.

Beth told her, and minutes later she called Beth over to her desk. "I have your aunt on the phone." She handed Beth the receiver.

"Aunt Camille?"

"Oh, honey! The nurse told me what happened. This is terrible. Are you all right?"

Her aunt's voice, so like Beth's mother's, made a huge lump swell in Beth's throat. "They won't let me see Mom or Dad," she managed to say.

"I'll come as soon as I can. Give me a few minutes to call the airport and see what I can arrange."

Beth's knees went weak with relief. Thirty minutes later her aunt had arranged a flight from Tampa to Chattanooga, and Jill Bledsoe had volunteered to meet her at the airport. Then there really was nothing to do but wait. Beth took a seat as close to the emergency room doors as possible, hoping she might catch a glimpse of her parents or Allie or Doug whenever the triage doors swung open. But she could see nothing, no one.

Beth's eyelids grew heavy as time passed. She fought sleep. She drank colas and forced half a sandwich down to please Faye. Sometime after midnight, the outside doors opened and her aunt Camille rushed into the room. Beth threw herself into her aunt's arms.

"Oh, Beth, honey, I got here as soon as I could."

Beth started crying uncontrollably and clung to her aunt. "They won't tell me anything, Aunt Camille. They won't let me see them. Please make them. Please!"

"Come with me." Camille walked with Beth to the receptionist desk. The staff had changed shifts, and Beth recognized no one, but they seemed to know all about her. "I want to know what's going on," her aunt said.

"Just a minute. I'll page Dr. Higdon."

Minutes later a tall man with glasses and a mop of curly black hair came out to meet them. He looked haggard. "I'm Dr. Higdon," he said.

"Camille Moffat. This is my niece, Beth Haxton. I'm her mother's sister. Please tell us what's going on."

"We have a more private room down the hall. Follow me."

Beth held her aunt's hand, and Faye went with them. The walk down the hall seemed endless. Once they were inside the small cubicle, Dr. Higdon said, "Please sit down."

"I don't want to sit," Beth said. She was angry at the doctor who'd kept her waiting so long.

"How are my sister and brother-in-law?" her aunt asked. "And their two children. Beth said they were in the accident too."

"Yes," the doctor said. "An ambulance brought in all four of them."

"I—I stayed home," Beth explained, although no one had asked her why she hadn't been in the van. "I had the flu."

"According to the police," the doctor said, "the van swerved from the road and careened down a hill, rolled over, and smashed into a tree. The impact was severe. The Jaws of Life had to be used to open the car and extract the passengers."

Beth shuddered. "B-But they're all right, aren't they? You fixed them up, didn't you?"

Dr. Higdon looked her in the eye. "No, Beth. They arrived at our emergency room DOA." His voice was soft, terribly soft.

"DOA?" Her voice quivered.

"Dead on arrival. I'm very sorry, but there was absolutely nothing we could do for them. Nothing at all. But I didn't feel you should be told this without a relative present."

5

Sunlight jabbed at Beth's closed eyelids. She turned her head, but the relentless rays of the sun wouldn't go away. Suddenly she felt her chest tighten and her breathing slow, then stop altogether. She felt as if she were drowning and began to flail her arms and legs like a swimmer kicking toward the surface. She crashed the surface and sat bolt upright, gasping for air, her eyes wide. She was in her bedroom. Pink and white flowers flecked the wallpaper. Pink carpet covered the floor. This was her room. Her room. She was safe. No . . . something was wrong.

The agony of the night before returned.

She had been told that her whole family was dead. Gone. Wiped out with a long skid, the squeal of tires, the impact of metal hitting a tree. Her last image of them haunted her: Allison bent over a book. Doug tossing his baseball. Her dad waving, her mother blowing a kiss. The tap on the horn at the end of the street. Now there was only silence in the big house. No sound of running water in the bathroom. No smell of brewing coffee. No muffled TV cartoons from the den. Silence, so ominous. She wanted to scream.

Dr. Higdon had given her and Aunt Camille sedatives. They had returned to Beth's house, where she had collapsed into a drugged, exhausted sleep. Beth threw back the covers and scrambled to her feet. She staggered, grabbed hold of the metal headboard of the bed, and fought to regain control of her ragged breath and thudding heart.

A knock on the door almost made her scream, *"Go away!"* Instead she rasped, "Come in."

Aunt Camille eased open the door. She was dressed in jeans and a T-shirt and her eyes looked puffy and red. "Jack and Terri are flying in today," she said.

I don't care, Beth thought. Jack and Terri were Camille's family. *Her family*. Beth didn't have a family anymore. "All right."

"Honey, we have to talk."

"I don't want to talk."

"Beth . . . we must. There are things that have to be decided."

"What things?"

Her aunt took a tissue from her jeans pocket. "We've got to plan a funeral." She sobbed into the tissue, but Beth felt strangely removed, as if she were watching a movie or a TV show. She didn't feel a part of the scene. Perhaps it would fade. Or go to snow like the end of a videotaped movie.

When her aunt regained her composure, Beth simply said, "I don't want to."

"We must. The story's in the paper, and people from your dad's company have been calling all morning. They want to send flowers. They want to pay their respects."

The idea seemed barbaric to Beth. She didn't want to think about a funeral. She didn't want to put her parents, her brother, and her sister into dark holes in the ground. She started to tremble. Her aunt reached for her. "We'll get through this, honey. We will."

Beth went into her aunt's arms, but the embrace felt odd to her, strangely out of kilter. She wasn't in her mother's arms. She pressed her lips together to stop the sobs struggling to get out. She lost the battle.

Teddy came over in the afternoon to stay with Beth while Faye took Camille to the airport to pick up Jack and Terri. Teddy sat on the edge of the sofa, his hands clamped tightly between his knobby knees. "I can't believe such a bad thing happened," he said. "It's not fair. It's not right."

Beth felt hollow, as if some giant hand had reached down and scooped out her insides, leaving only a shell. On the outside she was Beth Haxton. On the inside there was nothing. "I keep thinking Doug and Allison will come through the door arguing with each other," she said. "I keep thinking I'll wake up and this will have been a bad dream."

"More like a nightmare."

"You wake up from dreams and nightmares. But I'm not waking up from this, Teddy. I keep trying, but I can't."

He took her hand. His palm felt moist, clammy. He must have realized it because he quickly withdrew, wiped his hands on the cloth of his shorts, then picked up her hand again. "I wish there was something I could do for you."

"Just stick close to me. Through the funeral. Please. I—I don't want to fall apart."

"You're allowed."

She looked into his face. Teddy, her friend since kindergarten. His eyes looked dark and sad, his face pale in spite of the sunburn that streaked his nose and cheeks. "Did you have fun at Six Flags?"

"Yeah. We had a great time."

"Tell me about the rides. About every one of them."

"Are you sure? It's nothing."

She nodded vigorously. It was easier to talk about nothing than something. Because *something* was too terrible to discuss. Too dark and terrible to even think about.

"I'm really sorry, Beth." Terri stood just inside Beth's bedroom door, fidgeting with the ends of her dark hair.

"Everybody's sorry. But it doesn't change anything."

Terri chewed her lower lip. "Is there somebody you want me to call for you? You know, like a friend?"

"Everybody knows. Except Marcie. She's away on vacation." Beth wanted Marcie to know, but she had no way to tell her. She imagined her coming home and hearing. Marcie would cry, and Beth wanted to be there for her.

"This is the most awful thing to ever happen, Beth. I can't stop thinking about Allison and Doug. I keep thinking about the last time I saw them. I got into a fight with them, remember?"

Beth shook her head. Her brain felt fuzzy and numb, and remembering hurt her head. "Just drop it, Terri."

Terri took a step backward. "I'm sorry. I—I just don't know what to say."

"Please don't say anything, all right? It's just better if nobody says anything."

Terri nodded, but a minute later she asked, "Would you like something to eat? We could go downstairs. People have been bringing food over."

Beth whipped around. "I don't want anything! Do you hear me? I don't want to eat. I don't want to sleep. I just want everybody to leave me alone!"

Terri looked terror-stricken. "Well, gee, Beth. Okay. All right. I didn't mean to upset you. I—I was just trying to help."

"You can't help. No one can help." Fresh tears flooded Beth's eyes, surprising her. She'd thought she'd cried them all up by now. "Just go away. Please, Terri. Go away."

Terri backed out of the room. Beth threw herself across the bed, pounded the mattress with balled fists, and wept.

6

Beth dressed slowly, her fingers stiff and awkward. Soon the limo from the funeral home would be picking them up to take them to the church for the memorial service, then to the cemetery where she would watch her family be buried.

She had decided to wear her bright blue dress with white flowers. It had been her Easter dress, and she remembered the day she and her mother had shopped for it. "You look lovely," her mother had said. "You're growing up so fast. Honestly, before I turn around, we'll be shopping for your wedding dress."

"No, we won't, Mom," Beth said to her reflection as she dressed for the funeral. She would never shop with her mother again. She also knew that once the day was over, she'd never wear the dress again.

An hour later she entered the church with her aunt, uncle, and cousin. The pews were crowded, and at the front, on the wide steps of the cold stone altar, were four flower-draped caskets: two large mahogany ones, two smaller white ones. The caskets were closed, and a framed photograph had been placed on each of them. Throughout the service, Beth stared at the photos, absorbing, memorizing the familiar images, not wanting to ever forget the way they were. Allison's blond hair. Doug's toothy grin. Her father's intensely blue eyes. And her mother's high cheekbones and freckled nose.

Beth sat ramrod straight while the minister spoke about her family and how their bodies might be in the caskets but their souls were safe in heaven. The eulogies were punctuated by the quiet crying of the congregation, especially the sobs of her aunt and Terri. Beth struggled to keep her sobs inside. She wouldn't make a spectacle of herself by falling apart. Sunlight falling through the stained-glass windows cast colors over the caskets and flowers. The scene should have been pretty. It wasn't. It looked staged, as if some celestial lighting director had rigged the whole thing. Illusion . . . all was illusion. Even the organ music sounded forlorn and desolate. And no matter how hard Beth tried to think about God and heaven, she couldn't. It wasn't fair for God to take away her family, even if they were in heaven. She wanted them here on earth with her. What right did God have to take them? Didn't he know she loved them, needed them?

At the graveside, Beth stepped out of the car and into a smothering blanket of hot, muggy July air. She saw Teddy and his family, and he gave her an encouraging smile. She smiled bravely in return. The minister spoke again, and when everything was over, she stepped up to the caskets for a final farewell.

In the heat the flowers were wilting, their edges already turning brown. Beth pulled a single white rose from each of the four cascades. Her father had given her mother roses for Valentine's Day. But now their heavy perfume did not make Beth think of luscious bouquets and timeless love. This time they spoke to her of death.

She clutched the roses against her chest, turned and walked back to the limo, and settled in for the ride back to the house. Her family's house. The one she'd grown up in; the house she'd lived and laughed and cried in. She stared straight ahead, her mind blank and numb, her heart broken, heavy. All the light had gone out of her life. She didn't know how to get it back.

"Honey, we must talk."

"About what?" Three days had passed since the funeral. Beth had stayed in her room, eating food Camille brought her on trays, refusing to go to the table downstairs. Shut off in her room, she could pretend that the sounds she heard were from her parents. That the TV noise came from Doug's programs, not Terri's.

"Do you know what godparents are?" Camille asked, sitting on the side of Beth's bed and taking her niece's hand. "A godparent is someone who takes responsibility for another person's child at the child's baptism.

Jack and I are your godparents, and your parents—" She paused, composed herself. "Carol and Paul were Terri's godparents."

"So?"

"Not only are we godparents to one another's children, but we gave each other legal guardianship of each other's children in our wills."

"What does that mean?"

"It means that you belong to us now, Beth. We want to take you back to Tampa to live with us."

Move? She couldn't move. "B-But this is my home. I won't move away. You can't make me."

"You're only fourteen, a minor. Who will take care of you?"

Camille's voice was kind, but her questions made Beth feel cornered. She hadn't thought about her future. "I can take care of myself."

"Beth, I don't want this to be any harder than it already is. We're your family. We want you to live with us. You'll have a room of your own. We'll get all your furniture out of your old room to take with us—"

"But *this* is where I want to live. I don't want to move to Tampa."

Camille's hand tightened around Beth's. "I'm not trying to be cruel, Beth. I'm only trying to do what's best for you. Don't you understand? If you don't come with us, you'll have to go to a foster home. The courts won't let you live alone."

Beth pulled her hand from her aunt's. "What have they got to say about my life? Who do they think they are, anyway?"

"They make the rules, honey. Jack and I've been to see your father's attorney, and in your parents' will, everything is going to pass to you. But the legal process takes a long time, maybe a year or more. There'll be estate taxes and attorneys' fees." She waved her hand impatiently. "Just take my word for it. You can't stay here by yourself."

Fresh tears filled Beth's eyes. "You're saying I have no choice."

"I'm saying that Jack and Terri and I want you with us. We love you, Beth. You're family. You're all I have of my sister. I—I can't let you go."

Camille pulled Beth fiercely and protectively close. Beth kept her body rigid. Camille was her aunt, not her mother. Not ever her mother. She looked over her aunt's shoulder and saw Terri standing in the doorway. Her cousin's face was the color of chalk. Before Beth could move, Terri turned and skittered away, looking as if she'd been betrayed.

Beth had not been inside her parents' bedroom since before the accident. That evening, she passed the door and saw her aunt and Terri going through the closets. "What are you doing?" she cried, darting into the room.

"We have to put everything into storage," Camille said. "Jack's hiring a realtor to rent the house."

"But it's my house. I don't want somebody else living here."

"We must, Beth. Please try and understand. We have to get everything packed up and stored and your things ready for the move. Jack has to get back to work. We're renting a trailer for your stuff and leaving for Tampa in a week."

Beth felt as if she'd been assaulted. People

were making decisions about her life and she had no say in it. "This isn't fair!"

"I agree," Camille said, folding several of Carol's dresses and stacking them in a large box. "But there's *nothing* I can do to change what's happened. Don't you think I would if I could?"

Beth swiped at the hot tears collecting on her cheeks.

"Would you like to do some of this?" Camille asked. "Believe it or not, it helps." She caressed the folded dresses lovingly.

How could Beth pack up her mother's and father's lives and cram them into stiff brown boxes? In a heap on the floor, she saw her father's ratty old shirt and picked it up. She rubbed the worn, soft fabric against her cheek, caught the scent of his aftershave, and, shaking her head, said, "No. I don't want to do this."

Still clutching the shirt, she backed out of the room. Her father was gone . . . gone. And he was never coming home again.

7

"So you're moving tomorrow?" Teddy rested the basketball on his hip.

Beth, sitting on the stone wall that edged the driveway, stared down at the ground. "Yes. Some of Dad's friends are coming over to help Jack load the trailer with my stuff tonight. Then we'll go right after we get up and get ready."

"Bummer." Teddy bounced the ball several times. "I guess you won't even get to tell Marcie goodbye."

"Guess not."

"I'll tell her for you."

"Tell her I'll write. And e-mail. And I'll call too. Jack and Camille won't keep me from staying in touch with my friends."

"You think they'd try?"

Beth shook her head, slightly ashamed. "They'll pretty much do anything for me. Except let me stay here by myself."

"My mom asked if you could live with us."

Beth's raised her head. "She did?"

"She told your aunt you could stay all through high school and go down to Tampa in the summers. But your aunt said you belonged with your family and that since you were starting ninth grade at a new school in the fall, it wouldn't matter if you started it down there."

Beth, Teddy, and Marcie were all due to begin classes at Red Bank High School. "Except that I'll know a lot of the kids at Red Bank, and I won't know anybody at the school in Tampa."

"Mom told her that. Your aunt said you could hang out with Terri and her friends."

"Oh, thrill," Beth said in a flat voice. "As if Terri even has any friends."

"How are you getting along with Terri?"

Beth shrugged. "She stays out of my way. We haven't talked much."

"I guess she doesn't know what to say to you," Teddy suggested. "Her life's changing too, you know."

"What do you mean?"

"According to you, she's been a little princess with the castle all to herself all these years."

"True."

"Well, now you're moving in and it's Sharesville. Even her parents are yours now—sort of. I mean, she lost her aunt and uncle and two cousins. You're the only cousin she has in the world, Beth. The one and only." Teddy paused. "I don't want to upset you. Did I say too much?"

Beth grimaced. She hadn't thought about it that way before, but Teddy was right. Jack had no siblings, so she and Terri were the only cousins each would ever have. "Tell your mom thanks for the offer," Beth said. "I—I would have really liked to live with you-all."

"Sure," Teddy said. "You want to play

one last game of Horse? For old times' sake?"

Beth didn't. She just shook her head. "You write me, you hear?"

"I'll write."

"And don't make a pest of yourself with Marcie." Tears blurred Beth's eyes. "The two of you are my best friends in the whole world, and I'm going to miss you like crazy."

"Me too," Teddy mumbled. He walked over, pulled Beth to her feet, and put his arms around her.

She began to cry but held on tight, the way a drowning person would hold on to a rope in a wind-whipped lake.

"The car's packed and ready," Jack said, coming into the kitchen.

Beth looked up at him. "Already?"

Her uncle put his arm around her shoulder. "I'm sorry, honey. I wish there was some other way. I wish none of this had happened."

Teddy's father would help get the contents of the house into storage once they were gone, and a realtor would begin showing the house to prospective renters as soon as it was cleaned and painted. Beth nodded, not trusting her voice. She felt like a condemned prisoner.

Outside, the trailer containing all her bedroom furniture, books, clothes, pictures, and keepsakes had been hooked to a rental car for the ten-hour drive to Tampa. Her memories were in there—her very life was packed into that trailer. What was left of it, anyway.

Teddy and his family gathered on the driveway, and they all hugged goodbye. "I'll watch after your mother's flowers," Faye said.

"That would be nice," Beth said. "Mom liked her flowers a lot."

She struggled to hold back tears as she climbed into the backseat, where Terri was already settled in, her nose in a teen magazine, a wad of gum in her mouth. Terri blew a bubble, popped it, and kept reading. Beth plopped her bed pillow between them like an imaginary line. *Don't cross over*, it said.

"You want anything?" Aunt Camille asked from the front seat.

Beth shook her head.

Uncle Jack backed out of the driveway, tooted his horn, and waved to the Carpenters. Beth gazed out at her neighborhood sliding past the car window like photos in an album. All the pretty houses, in neat, orderly rows. And the trees, lush and green with summer leaves. Beth had spent almost fourteen summers in this place. Her lifetime.

Jack drove down Signal Mountain and across the Tennessee River and merged into traffic on the expressway. When the car moved onto Interstate 75, Beth saw a sign announcing that Atlanta was 103 miles away. In the distance, the foothills looked blue and hazy, the sky a murky bluish gray.

Against the sky, in her mind's eye, Beth saw the faces of her mother, father, Allison, and Doug as they had looked on the day they left for the picnic. She was going off to a new life, leaving them behind, just as death had left her behind when it had taken them.

Beth slipped on her sunglasses, hoping to shield her eyes, not from the glare of the sun, but from the stares of passing motorists. For surely they might wonder why a girl who looked for all the world as if she were headed off on vacation with her family was sitting in the backseat crying hard.

WINTER

8

Hey Marcie,

I know I'm e-mailing you every day, but you're my only friend, and I really miss you. I miss home too. And Teddy (but don't tell him—it'll go to his fat head) <bg> I've been living with my aunt and uncle for over a month, and I still can't get used to it. Uncle Jack travels a lot on business. Sometimes he leaves on Monday and doesn't come back until Friday. (My dad was home every night, remember?) So, we eat a lot of dinners without him. Terri and Aunt Camille argue, which makes me crazy. I want to tell Terri, "Shut up, already! Don't you know

how lucky you are to have a mother?" I
stay in my room as much as I can, but Aunt
Camille is always dragging me and Terri
someplace. She says I need to get out
more. As if!

I was wrong about Terri having no
friends. She has two, LuAnne and Kasey.
They're a lot like Terri. They giggle a lot and
talk about boys ALL the time. When school
starts next week, I plan to stay as far from
them as possible. Which is another thing.
I'll be going to Westwood Jr. High. They do
things different down here. No middle
schools, but jr. highs and high schools.
Wish I could start 9th grade in high school
like back home.

When you wrote about shopping for
school clothes, it made me cry. Mom
should be shopping with me. I keep remembering last year and all. Who'd have
ever guessed that it would be my last
shopping trip ever with my mother?

I know Aunt Camille is trying hard to help
me be happy here, but all I want to do is go
home. I want things back the way they
used to be. Got to sign off now, but I'll write

again tomorrow. Unless I think of something else I have to tell you today.<vbg>

Bye for now. And go hug your mother.

Beth clicked on the Send E-mail button just as there was a knock on her bedroom door. "I'm busy," she called.

"I want to ask you something." It was Terri. "It's important."

Reluctantly Beth opened the door. "What is it?"

Terri entered, her gaze darting everywhere. "Um—my friend LuAnne is having a pool party Saturday night and she wants us to come."

"I don't want to go."

"Why not?"

"I don't feel like partying." Beth turned away.

"It's the last party before school starts. Everyone will be there. It'll be fun."

"Fun for you, maybe, but not for me."

"How do you know?"

"I just know, that's all."

"You never want to do anything." Terri sounded pouty.

"Look, I just don't feel like going to some party. Don't you get it?"

"You could make friends." Terri's tone turned cajoling.

"I have friends. They just don't happen to live in Tampa."

Terri put her hands on her hips. "You have to make new friends, Beth. You live here now. This is your home."

Beth wanted to slap her. "I live here because I have to live here. But I don't like it one little bit."

Terri looked shocked. She took a step backward. "What's so horrible about living here? You've got everything you could want. All you have to do is say one word to my mother and she jumps to give you anything. I don't see what's so horrible about that."

"Would you like to trade places with me?"

Terri's cheeks colored, and she dropped her gaze. "No . . . I don't want to trade places with you. But I do want you to come to the party with me. The truth is if you don't go, I can't go. Mom won't let me go without you."

"Why didn't you tell me that in the first place?"

Terri shrugged. "I don't know."

"You know, Terri, if you'd just be honest with people, maybe you wouldn't have to argue about everything you want."

"I didn't think you'd go if you thought you were doing me a favor."

Exasperated, Beth shook her head. How little her cousin knew about her! "I'm not that way. I know how to be nice. I'm not above doing somebody—anybody—a favor."

"Even me?" Terri looked contrite.

"Yes," Beth said after a pause.

"Then you'll come to the party?"

With a start, Beth realized she'd painted herself into a corner. She still didn't want to go, but if she said no now, she'd come across as petty and mean. "Oh, all right," she mumbled after a long pause.

"Great." Terri was all smiles. "We'll have fun. We really will."

Terri sailed out of Beth's room, and Beth closed the door behind her. A sudden sadness overcame her. She shouldn't be going to parties. Not when neither Allison nor

Doug could ever attend one again. It wasn't right. Beth sagged onto the bed, tears pooling in her eyes. It wasn't right. It wasn't.

LuAnne's backyard swarmed with kids Beth didn't know and didn't want to meet. The pool and patio blazed with lights, and underwater swimmers took on distorted, rippled shapes. Hamburgers smoked on a massive grill, and a table overflowed with bowls of chips, cold drinks, salads, and desserts. Terri immediately locked onto Kasey, and Beth edged away from the crowds without being noticed.

At the far end of the backyard she found refuge beneath a large banyan tree. The tree's aerial roots hung down like the legs of a spider, and looking through them was like looking through the bars of a cage. With a heavy sigh, she leaned against one of the thicker root-trunks and kicked at the bare ground with the toe of her sandal. The sounds of splashing, laughter, and music coming from the party seemed offensive to her. How could everybody be so happy when she felt so sad and alone?

"Are you hiding on purpose, or did you just lose your way?"

Beth turned to see a boy approaching her. He balanced a paper plate of food in one hand. "I'll bet you're Beth."

"How do you know that?" He didn't look familiar.

"Word gets around. I'm Jared Harrison." He stopped in front of her and grinned. "And I've come to rescue you."

9

"Maybe I don't want to be rescued." Beth wished Jared would go away.

"Well then, you can rescue me. I hate these parties."

"Why'd you come?"

"Nothing better to do. Would you hold this for a minute?" He handed her his plate of food and pulled himself up onto a low branch of the banyan tree. He reached down for the plate. "Come on up. There's plenty of room." She hesitated. "Or you could go back to the party."

Beth struggled up onto the branch and

settled beside him. They weren't very high off the ground, but the new perspective made her feel better. She couldn't say why.

"Want a bite?" Jared offered his plate.

"I'm not hungry."

"I'm *always* hungry." He bit into his hamburger. "So, what are you doing this far from the party?"

"I don't feel much in a party mood."

"Yeah, I'll bet. I heard about your family."

"How?"

Jared gestured with his burger. "Terri told Kasey and LuAnne. They told everybody else."

"That's my personal business." It upset Beth so much to think that Terri and her friends had gossiped about her.

"Not when you're around the Mouth of the South. Or Terri the Tattler, as she's also sometimes known."

Beth smiled, feeling a perverse pleasure in her cousin's nicknames.

"I'm sorry about what happened to your parents," Jared said. "That's a pretty bad thing."

She hung her head. "Nobody understands."

"Maybe not about that, but I *do* understand what it feels like to be the new kid on the block." He munched on a chip. "My parents divorced a few years ago. Mom remarried when I was twelve and we moved here. So I was facing being the new kid in school two years ago, like you are now. Starting in a new school can be pretty awful, if you let it."

"I'm not looking forward to it." She glanced toward the party. The tree's leaves obscured her vision, but she imagined Terri huddled with her friends, blabbing on about some guy or her newest outfit. Sometimes it made Beth sick to her stomach.

"We're not such a bad bunch," Jared said. "Not everybody travels in groups. There are a few of us Lone Rangers around."

"You're a Lone Ranger?"

He saluted. "Let's just say I don't hang out with any group of kids in particular. I like everybody, and I hang out with anybody I feel like."

"You remind me of someone."

"Who?"

"A boy back home."

"Your boyfriend?"

"He's a boy and he's my friend. So I guess he's my boyfriend. But no, not in the way you mean. His name's Teddy and he lives— lived next door to me."

"I had a friend where I used to live too. Her name was Kelly. But I did like her as a girlfriend." Jared dropped his empty paper plate to the ground. "But what did I know? I was twelve." He laughed. "And by now I'm sure she's forgotten my name."

"I won't ever forget my friends," Beth said with emotion.

"You don't forget them, but they do sort of fade."

She didn't like the idea. If memories of her friends faded, what about memories of her family? "What about your real father? Has he faded away?"

"I miss him. My stepdad and I don't get along real well."

"I thought you liked everybody."

"Everybody under age twenty." He twisted toward her on the branch. "I wish I could see more of my real dad, but he's not around. Still, it's not like your situation."

"Actually, I've sort of worked out a scenario about my situation," she said. "I pretend that I'm only visiting my aunt and uncle and that my family is back home, all safe and happy. Sometimes it's just easier to pretend than it is to remember."

"I do that myself. Especially after my stepdad and I have a blowup. I go in my room and think back to when Dad and Mom were still married. It wasn't paradise, but I remember being happier when we were all together."

"Sometimes I wonder if I'll ever be happy again."

"Sure you will." He slid off the branch, turned, and reached up for her. "Tell you what, I'll make it my mission to see that you are." He placed his hands firmly around her waist and pulled her down toward him.

"You don't have to," she said. They were so close, she could feel his breath on her cheek.

"I know." He stepped back, bent, and picked up the plate he'd tossed down. "But no one should have to face entry into Westwood *and* Terri the Tattler without some sort of safety net.''

She laughed and was surprised at how good it felt to laugh again. ''Thanks,'' she told him.

''For what?''

''For making me laugh.''

He bowed from the waist. ''It's a Harrison specialty. Just ask any of my teachers. Want to go back to the party with me?''

She shook her head. ''Thanks, but no thanks.''

''Then I'll see you at school come Monday.''

''Sure,'' she said. ''Come Monday.'' She watched him return to the patio alone.

''Where did you disappear to?'' It was Terri's first question when they arrived home from the party that night. ''I looked for you everyplace to introduce you around.''

''I sort of hung out with a tree in the backyard.''

Terri stared at Beth as if she'd lost her mind. ''You could have had a good time, you know. You didn't have to hide.''

"I had an okay time."

"I wanted to point out Jared Harrison to you."

Beth's head snapped up. "Why?"

A gooey smile spread over Terri's face. "I have plans for him and me."

"Plans?"

"Absolutely. I think he's totally buff, and this year I intend to make him my guy. Count on it."

10

◆◆◆◆◆

The halls of Westwood were clogged with students returning for classes, and when the tardy bell rang, Beth was still lost in the halls where Terri had abandoned her. "Meet me at the front door at three-fifteen," Terri had yelled before speeding away. Beth finally found her way to homeroom, where she received a reprimand from her teacher for being late. At lunch she sat by herself. She was poking at her meal halfheartedly when Jared Harrison plunked his lunch tray next to hers.

"Want some company?" he asked.

"Sit only if you want to face social ostracism."

"Things can't be that bad."

She wanted to tell somebody how much she missed her friends—and her former life—but she couldn't find the words. Plus, she was afraid she'd burst into tears and make a spectacle of herself. "Things are just different," she wound up saying.

"Show me your class schedule. Maybe we'll have a class together." She showed him her card. "Sixth-period algebra." He handed it back. "We can sit together."

The knowledge calmed her. At least his was one friendly face. "*If* I survive until then."

"You'll make it. You have to. I don't want to face Sheffield by myself."

"Is she tough?"

He snorted. "You could say that."

Beth's heart sank. She was having trouble concentrating in classes already. How was she ever going to make it through a really rough one? "Maybe I could drop it."

"What—and leave me to fight the Lion all by myself?"

He looked panicked, and it made her smile. "Okay—I'll give it a try."

The bell rang, and he stood. "I got to run. Literally. Phys ed next period. Nice to see you again, Beth."

She ducked into the bathroom and brushed her long brown hair. Just seeing Jared had brightened her day considerably, and now she could look forward to seeing him again in class.

Behind her a bathroom stall door opened, and a girl's image flashed in the mirror. She was about Beth's height, but waif thin. Her short hair stood up in spikes in a bright shade of orange that matched her lipstick. A line of stud earrings followed the curve of each ear, and a nose ring jutted from one nostril. The girl wore a short denim skirt, a denim vest, and a black tank top. On her upper left arm, Beth saw a crude heart-shaped tattoo. The girl dropped a duffel bag to the floor and stepped up to the sink, where she bent and splashed water on her face. When she raised her head, she caught Beth's gaze in the mirror and snarled, "Something bothering you?"

"Uh—no."

"Then stop staring."

Beth glanced away, but when the girl leaned closer to the mirror and tucked her nose ring into her nostril and out of sight, Beth gawked again.

"I told you to get out of my face!"

Beth didn't need a second warning. She snatched up her books and ran from the bathroom and the belligerent, weird-looking girl.

In algebra class, Jared signaled to her from the back of the room, and she hurried to the seat he'd saved for her. She took copious notes when Mrs. Sheffield detailed what was expected, and only looked up when the final bell rang.

Jared waited while Beth gathered her things. "I'm exhausted from watching you take notes," he said.

"I don't want to get behind."

"Catching the bus home?"

"Not today. Aunt Camille insisted on picking us up on the first day. We're meeting out front."

"Come on. I'll walk with you."

She felt less intimidated walking alongside

Jared in the crowded, noisy halls. Once outside, she looked around for Terri. "Guess she's late."

"I'll wait with you. Let's sit." A stone bench beneath a large tree offered shade from the hot afternoon sun. Cars and buses lined up in the loading zone. "Day one is over," he said. "You'll never have to go through it again."

"I'll remind myself of that tomorrow when I'm still lost wandering the halls."

Just then a motorcycle roared around a waiting bus and screeched to a stop almost in front of the bench. A guy dressed in torn jeans and a black T-shirt balanced the sleek cycle and gunned the big engine. The girl with orange hair and an attitude flopped her duffel bag onto the seat, put on a helmet, and swung onto the bike behind the driver. He glanced over his shoulder once before revving the engine and speeding off. "Who's *she*?" Beth asked.

"Sloane Alonso."

"You know her?"

"Everybody knows Sloane."

Beth made a face. "She's scary."

"She's all right."

"You *like* her?"

"I told you, I like everybody."

"Really? She's so different from the other kids I've met."

"She's got problems."

"Such as?"

"Rotten home life. The worst. When things get really bad, she's been known to bring a sleeping bag and crash here at the school."

"You're joking." But Beth could tell by his expression that he wasn't. "Where does she sleep?"

"Girls' bathrooms, janitors' closets, anyplace she can sneak into without getting caught."

"And nobody knows? Not the principal, or a teacher?"

"Nobody knows and everybody knows, if you get my meaning. There are a lot of rumors. If she gets caught, she'll be suspended."

"Why doesn't she just let somebody in authority know about her rotten home life?"

" 'Cause she'd probably get sent to some foster home."

"Seems like that would be better than living the way she does."

"She doesn't think so. Some of us help her out. We bring her food. Keep our mouths shut."

Beth held her breath. Was he asking her not to tell anyone? "It's none of my business."

Jared grinned amiably. "I figured you for the type to keep a secret. Not like your cousin."

"What did Terri do to Sloane?"

"Ratted on her once. Got her into trouble. Terri didn't have to, but she did. It really bummed a lot of us out."

"Is that why kids don't like Terri?"

Jared shrugged. "There are lots of things about Terri that put kids off. She carries around this 'I'm better than you' attitude. I don't mean to slam her. I know she's your cousin and all."

"No problem." Beth knew exactly what Jared meant. In the weeks she'd lived with Terri, Beth had felt no special affection for her cousin. Terri had an abrasive quality—not like Sloane's, but like a thornbush that repelled closeness. "Do *you* feed Sloane?"

"Sure. It's the least I can do for her."

"Is that guy on the motorcycle her boy-friend?"

"I guess. He's new from the one she had last school year. She always dates older guys. Mostly because they can drive." He draped his elbows over the back of the bench. "Which is my main goal. I can't wait until I can drive unrestricted."

Her fifteenth birthday was in March, so she had a long time before she'd be sixteen and driving. A long time before she could return home on her own. "One day you'll drive this baby to the mall without me," her father had joked the day he'd brought the van home from the car lot. And she'd rolled her eyes and groaned, "No way! It's ugly. If my friends see me in this, I'll die!" Except that she hadn't died. Her family had.

"Excuse me." Jared snapped his fingers in front of her face. "Is it something I said, or do you just check out on people?"

"Sorry." Embarrassed, she stood. She hadn't expected to be blindsided by such an innocent memory.

Terri, rushing up, saved her from having to explain. "Sorry I'm late, but I got to talking—'' She stopped abruptly when she saw Jared.

He rose and grabbed his books. "Catch you tomorrow."

He walked away. Terri grabbed Beth's arm. "All right, *cousin*. Just what do you think you're doing?"

11

"What's that supposed to mean?" Beth asked.

"I told you at the party I liked Jared. I thought you understood that he was 'hands off.' "

"But I wasn't—"

"I *saw* you sitting here making friendly with him." Terri's face had turned red, and her eyes narrowed.

Beth almost lost her patience and blasted Terri, but a car's horn interrupted her.

"Over here!" Aunt Camille called, waving.

"This isn't over," Terri hissed as the two

of them hurried to the car. Beth settled in the backseat, and Terri took the front.

"I know I'm late, but I got hung up at a meeting," Aunt Camille said. "Hope you haven't been waiting too long." When neither girl answered, Camille asked Beth, "How was your first day?"

"Aren't you going to ask about *my* day?" Terri asked before Beth could answer.

"Well, of course. But you've done this before at Westwood. Beth hasn't." Camille caught Beth's eye in the rearview mirror. "So tell me about it. Do you like your classes? Did you find your way around easily? Meet any interesting new kids?"

"Yes. No. Yes."

"Okay, I promise not to badger you. I'm not trying to pry, honey. I'm only trying to make sure you're happy."

How could Beth tell her that she wasn't happy? That she didn't know how to be happy anymore?

"Tell you what," Camille said. "Since Jack's on the road, why don't we go out for dinner? Chinese all right?"

Beth and Terri agreed, but once they'd been served their food, Beth could hardly swallow it. She kept remembering every other first day of school in her life. How she and her brother and sister sat around the table and took turns telling about their new classes. And how Doug and Allison always argued over who went first. And how their mother would have made one of their special desserts. Last year she'd baked a chocolate cake with white icing—Allison's favorite.

"You're not eating much," Aunt Camille said to Beth.

"I'm not real hungry."

"No matter. We'll take it home."

Home. If only, Beth thought.

That night Beth had an e-mail from Marcie.

Hi Beth—

Geez, what a day. Red Bank HS is like, HUGE. And incoming freshmen are the lowest life-form in the universe. I was late to every class. I have English in one end of the building and phys ed in the opposite end. There's no way I can make it over there and change to my gym clothes in time. I'm doomed to be late.

I don't have a single class with anybody I know and only ran into Teddy at the bus stop after school. We decided that we'll give it just two weeks and if it doesn't get better, we're dropping out! <bg> It goes without saying that we both miss you. But Teddy surprised me and asked me to sit with him at the first football game Friday night. If you were here, the three of us would go. But you're not here.

Teddy says the renters in your house have four kids—all under ten! And they pester him all the time. Please write and tell me how the first day went for you. Hope it was better than mine.

Beth felt renewed homesickness. Still, she had to admit that her first day hadn't been as horrible as Marcie's. Ninth-graders were at the top of the food chain at Westwood, so she wouldn't have to hit the bottom until next year. That was a good thing. And then there was Jared. He was a good thing too.

Terri walked into Beth's room uninvited.

"If you came to yell at me again, go away," Beth said.

"My friends have been calling, asking about you and Jared," Terri blurted out. "Everybody saw the two of you sitting together. They know I like him and they want to know what's going on."

"There is no 'me and Jared.' Where do people get such crazy ideas?"

"Because you were seen together. It made a statement."

Beth shook her head. "That's the dumbest thing I ever heard. If I'd been sitting there with Santa Claus would everybody have thought I had something going on with him?"

The idea must have struck Terri as funny, because she snickered.

Beth added, "For the record, I think Jared spoke to me because he knows what it feels like to be the new kid in school. He was just being nice."

Terri looked glum. "He's nice, all right. But nothing I do makes him notice me."

Beth didn't know what to say. She could hardly tell Terri what Jared really thought about her. "I also ran into some girl named Sloane, and Jared was telling me about her," Beth remarked, changing the subject.

Terri's eyes widened. "Stay clear of her. She's bad news. Nothing but trouble with a capital *T*."

"Why do you say that?"

"Just look at her. She dresses like a refugee from a punk rock band, not to mention her tattoo. She's supposed to keep her arm covered during school hours, but she doesn't. Plus she's dumb."

"Dumb?"

"You know, she's in the retard class. If you care about your reputation, not to mention your *life*, stay clear of Sloane."

"But Jared was telling me that her home life is the pits and that she hides in the bathrooms to keep from going home at night. That she sleeps in closets and bathroom stalls. Is it true?"

Terri looked unmoved by Sloane's plight. "She doesn't do it all that often. Some of the kids think it's cool, some think it's creepy. But nobody tells on her. I made a mistake of telling a teacher she was smoking in the bathroom way back in seventh grade, and she's never gotten over it. Believe me, I stay out of her way. You should too."

"Isn't there anyone who could help her?"

"She doesn't want help. And who's going to take a chance and cross her? Not me." Terri's eyes narrowed. "And you shouldn't either, if that's what you're thinking. Don't go sticking your nose where it doesn't belong, Beth."

With that warning, Terri left the room.

Beth awoke in the night hungry. Her leftover Chinese food was in the refrigerator, so she quietly went into the kitchen, retrieved it, and began to eat it cold from the carton at the breakfast bar. The glow from the plug-in night-lights cast shadows, and the moon shone through the bay window, spilling a silvery glow on the smooth floor. Silence. All around her, silence.

The kitchen was spacious, with polished white cabinets and tidy countertops. No dish towels dropped haphazardly. Her mother's kitchen counters had held a set of chipped ceramic canisters and, beside the stove, a glass jar filled with cooking utensils.

There were always boxes that had never made it back to the pantry, and plastic cups and mismatched mugs of half-drunk coffee. Her father always forgot where he put down his cup and poured himself another.

Camille's refrigerator was sleek and gleaming, free of fingerprints and smudges. In Beth's house, the refrigerator had been covered with sticky-notes, photographs, and a collection of Doug's magnetic alphabet letters. Her family sometimes spelled out messages or left nutty remarks. *The red dog forgot his lunch.* And *PTA meet bring bi$cuits*—the dollar sign used because there was only one *s*.

Until now, she'd never noticed how neat and clean Camille kept her kitchen. Tidy, orderly. And lifeless. Beth shivered. Her hunger disappeared. She walked swiftly to the garbage can and dumped the carton of food. She carefully stepped around the puddle of cold moonlight and hurried back up to her room.

12

◆◆◆◆◆

Teddy—
Wow, was it ever great to hear from you. If you're at Marcie's sending me e-mail, what else are you doing with my best friend? (Yes, you're still my best friend, Marcie. The only person I really like down here is Jared, but it's not like you and me. I see him at school. He doesn't call.)

Wish I could be up there with you-all for Thanksgiving. Aunt Camille asked me what I'd like her to cook special. As if I care what we eat. I'm still pretending like I'm visiting, and not living here. It makes it easier.

School's a drag, everybody's ready to

bust out. And it's still pretty warm, so it hardly seems like November. Bet you've already had the fireplace going, haven't you? I remember last year and the big storm and losing power and roasting marshmallows over the fire.

The weirdest thing happened last week. I was passing a playground and I looked over and saw this little girl on the swings. Her back was to me, but she had long blond hair and she was wearing a red shirt and a red hairband. I kept watching her and all of a sudden it was like time moved backward and I heard Allison's voice say: "Push me higher, Beth! Higher!"

And I heard myself say, "I'm tired of pushing you. Learn how to pump your legs, Allison. I can't push you forever."

And I kept thinking, Allison! Allison! And all of a sudden I yelled, "Allison!"

The girl on the swing stopped and turned. She looked right at me. Then she jumped off the swing and ran away. I shouted for her to stop, that I didn't mean to scare her, but she kept going. I don't blame her. She probably thought I was crazy. Maybe I am. But for a minute, she was Allison and I was teaching her how to pump her legs. I DID teach my sister how to swing, you know. I don't know what got into me that day, but I hope the girl wasn't too freaked.

I'd never tell anybody except you guys about this. Sometimes I think I see Allison or Doug in a crowd at the mall. But, of course, I don't. It's not real. It's never real.

On the Wednesday before Thanksgiving break, Beth whipped into the bathroom after lunch and collided with Sloane Alonso.

"Hey, watch where you're going!"

Beth staggered backward. "Sorry."

Sloane stooped down to retrieve the contents of her purse, which had spilled across the tiled floor. It looked as if her purse held everything she owned. Beth knelt to help.

"I can do it." Sloane grabbed her mascara from Beth's hand.

Beth stared. Sloane's lip was swollen, and one of her eyes looked bruised. "What happened?" Beth blurted out the words before she could stop herself.

"None of your business." Sloane stuffed makeup into her purse and stood. "I told you once before not to stare at me. Don't make me repeat myself."

Beth saw a duffel bag and a rolled-up sleeping bag propped against the wall. Her heart thudded. "Is that your stuff?"

"Yeah, it's mine. Leave it alone." Sloane rose and tossed her purse over her shoulder.

"Are you just going to leave it there?"

"Who are you, the bathroom police?"

"I—I just wondered if it was safe."

Sloane stepped closer, glaring at Beth. "It's safe. Everybody knows to leave my stuff alone. And you should know it too."

"I'm not going to mess with your stuff."

"Good." Sloane stepped around Beth.

"Are you spending Thanksgiving with someone?"

Sloane paused and gave Beth a cold stare. "Yeah. I'm going to Grandma's."

The tardy bell rang, and Sloane muttered a curse word. "I better not get a detention because of you." She shoved past Beth and fled the bathroom.

Beth didn't move. Slowly the truth dawned on her. *Sloane had plans to spend the night in the school bathroom!* She chewed on her bottom lip. Should she tell somebody and risk Sloane's fury? It was a big risk. *Jared!* Yes, she'd ask Jared.

She squirmed through algebra class, and the second the bell rang, she seized Jared's arm and dragged him into the hall. She told him her suspicions and ended by asking, "What should I do? Hurry—my aunt's picking us up today, so I've got about ten minutes to figure out how to handle this."

"I think you should stay out of it."

"But why? It isn't right to spend the night in a sleeping bag in the school bathroom."

"Why do you care?"

"I don't know," Beth answered honestly. "It—It just isn't right! Someone should *do* something."

"Maybe she's going to meet her boyfriend and spend the weekend with him."

His explanation, so stunningly simple, made Beth feel stupid. "I—I didn't think of that."

Jared shrugged. "I don't know what she's doing. But if she wanted it to be your business, she would have told you."

"She said something about Grandma's, but I thought she was just being sarcastic."

"She probably was." He shifted his books. "Look, Beth, you don't know what's going on and I don't think you should get involved. Sloane knows what she's doing."

Jared was right. She was better off staying out of Sloane's life. "Okay, you've convinced me." By now the halls were practically empty. "I should get of out here."

As she hurried away he called, "Have a nice Thanksgiving."

"You too." She didn't look back.

She was passing the bathroom where Sloane's stuff was stashed when she heard voices. Beth stepped inside and saw Mrs. Olsen, Beth's homeroom teacher, confronting Sloane. "Answer me," Mrs. Olsen was demanding. "What are you hiding in this bathroom, Ms. Alonso?"

"Can't a person stash her stuff without everybody becoming unglued?" Sloane answered crossly.

"Are you ready?" The words were out of Beth's mouth before she could stop them.

Mrs. Olsen and Sloane turned. "Ready?" Sloane asked.

"Ready to leave. My aunt's waiting out front."

Mrs. Olsen looked positively shocked. "Is Sloane going home with *you*, Beth?"

"Um, sure." Beth smiled. Sloane glared. "Sorry I'm a little late, but I got to talking after class," Beth added.

"I never dreamed . . . I mean, I had no idea the two of you were friends." Mrs. Olsen said.

"Sure," Beth said. "And I invited her for the Thanksgiving holiday. That's why she's got all her stuff. She's staying with me for a few days."

"Well . . . if you say so . . ."

"Come on," Beth urged Sloane. "Can't keep my aunt and Terri waiting."

Sloane reached down and scooped up her duffel and sleeping bag. Beth breezed out of the bathroom and down the hall toward the main entrance. She was almost at the door when Sloane caught up with her and grabbed her arm. "Just a minute, girl."

Beth took a deep breath and turned to face her. "What?"

"Just what do you think you're doing?"

"Taking you home with me for the

Thanksgiving holiday," Beth said, suddenly irked by Sloane's attitude. "And trying to save your butt. Are you coming? Or do you really want to spend Thanksgiving in the girls' bathroom?"

13

◆◆◆◆◆

Sloane's hostile expression softened. "Listen, you did a good job of getting me off the hook in there, but I don't want to go home with you."

"What else are you doing for Thanksgiving?"

"I got plans," Sloane insisted.

"Well, you'd better change them. At least temporarily. Mrs. Olsen's watching us from the doorway. You'd better come with me to my aunt's car."

Sloane nodded. "Okay, so I'll ride to the corner and get out."

"My aunt won't go for that."

Sloane gave a disgusted grunt. "I won't hang around Terri the Twit's house all weekend."

Beth suppressed a smile. *Twit*. Another endearing name for her cousin. "Suit yourself, but for tonight you're stuck at our place."

Sloane muttered a few swear words. Beth shuffled her books and picked up Sloane's duffel bag. As they walked toward Camille's car, Sloane asked, "You're Terri's cousin, aren't you? I heard about you. And I guess we've got some things in common."

"What things?"

"Like you, I've had some bad breaks. A crummy life. And crappy parents." Sloane hoisted her sleeping bag. She had no books. "Can you think of something worse than crappy parents?"

Beth looked at her over her shoulder. "Yeah. Dead ones."

As they approached the car, Terri gaped out the passenger side window. Beth pulled open the back door. "Aunt Camille, I know this is short notice, but I've decided to bring a friend home for the weekend."

Terri almost choked.

Camille looked surprised, but she recovered quickly. "Well, of course. Certainly." She eyed Sloane speculatively. "Any friend of Beth's is welcome."

"This is Sloane Alonso. She's . . ." Beth realized she didn't have anything else to add.

Sloane slid across the seat. "She's glad to meet you," she said, finishing Beth's sentence, her demeanor changing chameleon-like from rude to sweet, almost gushing.

"And your family doesn't mind if you spend the holiday with us?"

"They don't mind." Sloane gave Terri a smirk, then settled in the seat as if she owned it.

Beth refused to meet Terri's gaze. Beth felt a bit light-headed. She'd seized control of a situation and bent it to her will. She hadn't felt so daring since before her parents' accident.

"Nice place." Sloane tossed her gear on Beth's floor and assessed the bedroom.

Beth's glow was beginning to wear off. What was she going to do with Sloane for four whole days? They had nothing in common, and Sloane was a known troublemaker. What if she stole something from Beth's aunt and uncle's house? "You—um—want anything?"

"Got anything to eat?"

"In the kitchen."

"Could I take a shower first?"

"My bathroom's across the hall." Beth gestured.

"*Your* bathroom?"

"Terri has her own in her room." Sloane made a face, and Beth realized individual bathrooms must sound pretentious to a girl who took food handouts from her classmates. "So, I'll bring you a snack." Beth hurried to the kitchen, where her aunt and Terri were waiting to pounce on her.

"Just what do you think you're doing?" Terri fired at her.

Beth headed for the refrigerator. "I invited a friend home for the holidays. What's the big deal?" She glanced at her aunt. "Both of you've been after me to get some friends."

"Well, you didn't have to pick the worst girl in the school, did you?"

"Terri, that's enough!" Aunt Camille turned to Beth. "I don't mind your having a friend over, honey, but next time I'd like a little more notice."

Beth's smile was conciliatory. "You're right, Aunt Camille. I should have asked, but it happened kind of suddenly. I think Sloane's parents are out of town and Sloane was supposed to stay with another girl, but the plans got all messed up and she didn't have anyplace to go. Instead of letting her stay alone at her house all weekend, I invited her here. I'm sorry I didn't check it out with you first, but there was no time. They were closing up the school and so I just invited her." Beth's mouth went dry. She didn't like lying, but couldn't possibly have sorted out the truth for her aunt.

"I can't believe this!" Terri exclaimed.

"It's all right," Camille insisted. "I want you to feel free to bring your friends here." Terri dropped dramatically into a chair. Camille said, "Lighten up, Terri. Sure Sloane doesn't look like all *your* friends, but I expect you to make her feel welcome." She glanced at the kitchen clock. "Listen, I have to run to the store for a few last-minute things. Dinner doesn't just crawl onto the table unassisted, you know." She picked up her car keys. "I'll be back soon."

As the door closed behind her mother, Terri shot off the chair. "I can't believe you brought that girl to my house!"

"She's here. Believe it."

"What were you thinking?"

"I was thinking that she didn't need to be spending Thanksgiving hiding out in some school bathroom. I was thinking that I would be nice to her and offer her a place to stay. Sorry if you don't agree."

Terri crossed her arms. "Well, don't expect me to entertain her. Me and my friends are going to the mall first thing Friday morning. We were planning on taking you, but now you can just stay here with your new buddy."

"No problem. I don't like being with you and your geeky friends anyway."

"My friends aren't geeks! And tonight, plus every minute *she's* here, I'm locking my bedroom door. In case she decides to murder us all in our sleep."

"Get a grip."

"Oh, drop dead!"

Beth counted to ten, and once she'd calmed down, she returned to her room balancing a tray heaped with crackers, peanut butter, grapes, and a bag of cookies. The bathroom door was open, and steam from Sloane's shower blanketed the hallway. With both hands full, Beth poked the door of her bedroom open with her toe. It swung inward silently. She saw Sloane, wrapped in a towel with her back turned, sorting through Beth's closet as if she were in a department store instead of somebody's private room.

All Terri's dire warnings bombarded Beth. With her heart hammering, she asked, "Need some help, Sloane?"

14

◆◆◆◆◆

Without a hint of embarrassment at being caught pawing through Beth's clothes, Sloane said, "I was looking for something to wear."

Beth set down the tray. "What's the matter with your clothes?"

Sloane eyed the duffel bag sitting on the floor. "I didn't have time to do the laundry before I left home. Besides, the machines in my apartment building are all busted anyway."

With her hair slicked back and wet from the shower, her thin, jutting shoulders showing above the towel, and her face free of makeup, she looked childlike and vulnerable. Beth could more plainly see the dark smudge of a bruise beneath her eye and the puffiness of her lip. She saw another bruise on her arm and yet another on her leg. "Why *did* you leave home?"

"Are you writing a book?"

"No. But I sort of made up a fib to my aunt, and now I'd like to know. Just for me."

Sloane shrugged, saw the tray of food, and went for it. She spread peanut butter on several crackers and talked between bites. "My old man and me don't get along. He thinks I'm a slut."

"He calls you that?" The word shocked Beth.

"He calls me a lot of things. Especially when he's boozing. Mostly I try and stay out of his way, but sometimes we get into it."

"What about your mom?"

"She drinks right along with him. And he hits her. So sometimes I can't stand to hear him beating on her and I get between them to try and make him stop. Which really makes him mad. So I get a few licks too."

"You've had it rough."

"Who hasn't? It's just luck of the draw—I got the family I got, you got the one you got. Terri gets to live like some princess. Life ain't fair."

Beth couldn't imagine living the way Sloane did. She thought of her own father, quiet and gentle. He'd never so much as spanked her, Allison, or Doug. A pang of longing stabbed her. Fighting tears, she went to her closet and began shoving aside hangers. "I didn't see your boyfriend today. Doesn't he usually pick you up?"

"Carl's out of town. He's got this uncle up in Alabama who owns this garage. Anyway, his uncle is helping him trade in his cycle for a car. I'm going to miss that cycle."

Beth pulled out some jeans and a clean T-shirt. "These should probably fit." She was taller than Sloane and not as slim, but the jeans were a pair she'd outgrown. "You can keep them."

"I don't want charity. I'll get them back to you after I wash."

"Would you like to do some laundry now? You can use our machine."

"I could throw in some stuff. Sure, that'll

be fine." Sloane tugged on the borrowed clothes, picked up her bag, and asked, "Which way?"

Once the clothes were started, they went to the kitchen, where Camille, home from the store, was busy preparing supper. "We'll be eating in about an hour," she said. "Jack's firing up the grill right now." She glanced at Sloane, then looked startled, and Beth realized that she was just now seeing the bruises on Sloane's face. "What happened?"

"I fell."

Beth cast her aunt a glance warning her not to press Sloane for details and was relieved when she didn't.

They ate dinner outside on the patio, their chairs snug around the table, looking for all the world like a family. Except that they weren't. The air felt soft and cool. The smell of charcoal and grilled burgers reminded Beth of the cookouts her family used to have with the Carpenters. Fourteen summers gone. Like smoke in the wind. Now she sat on a patio hundreds of miles from home, an orphan, amid relatives she didn't want to be with and a girl stranger than anyone she'd ever known. Life wasn't fair. Sloane was certainly right about that much.

Beth let Sloane sleep in on Thanksgiving Day. Camille and Terri were busy in the kitchen and Terri was acting hateful, so Beth went out to the garage, where she found her uncle sorting through boxes and organizing shelves. "You off KP duty?" he asked.

"I'm just in the way in the kitchen." Beth heaved a sigh, saw an empty spot, and sat.

"I know what you mean. Thought I'd hang around out here. And . . . I've been putting off this cleanup for ages. Now's as good a time as any." She watched him stack boxes. He opened one and gave a grunt. "Hey, come look at this and tell me what you see."

Beth peered inside. "Old clothes."

He shook out a set of army fatigues. "Not just any old clothes. This is my army gear. Your dad and I were in the same company, you know. Lived right next to each other in army housing. Your mom and Camille were pregnant at the same time."

"Mom told me."

Jack stroked the garments, put them aside, and pulled out a photo. "Boy, this was a long time ago."

He handed the picture to Beth, who took it and saw the images of Jack and her father standing next to a Jeep. Both men had shaved heads and wore big smiles. They looked young, slim, fit, and happy. A lump filled her throat, and the photo wavered as tears filled her eyes.

Jack gently took the photo and cradled it in his hand. "Paul was a good man. I miss him."

"Me too."

Jack smoothed her hair. "He was always on my case about my being on the road so much. He'd say, 'Get your priorities straight, Jack. You spend too much time away from your family.' And I'd say, 'I've got to feed them.' And he'd say, 'Yeah, but sometimes it's better to eat light than to get too much distance between you and them.' He once said, 'I never heard a man on his deathbed say he'd wished he'd worked more. On his deathbed, a man always wishes he'd spent more time with his wife and kids.' " Jack tucked the photo into his shirt pocket. "He turned down better-paying jobs so that he could spend more time with you all, you know."

She hadn't known, but she believed him. Jack's reminiscences sounded exactly like her father. He had always put his family first. They had done things together— school events, sports, games, travel. She'd been getting bored with it, wishing they didn't have quite so much togetherness. She'd been wanting to do more with her friends, less with her family. But it was all over now. She'd never be with her family again.

Jack looked at her. "I've depressed you. I'm sorry. I just got carried away. The truth is, I miss him too, Beth. Our family get-togethers every year were our chance to renew our friendship. I don't have anyone to talk to anymore. . . . Paul was a good friend."

Beth sniffed and wiped the moisture from her cheek. "It's okay. I'm all right."

Jack knelt and took her hands in his. "I feel honored to have known such a fine man as your father. And I'm proud to have you as my daughter. Heartsick about the circumstances that brought you here, but proud nonetheless.''

She managed a smile. ''Thanks.''

''We'll always take care of you, Beth. And for the record, I'm trying very hard to realign my priorities. I'm backing off my travel schedule after the first of the year.'' He wiped her cheek with his thumb. ''Your father would have been pleased. Yes—Paul would think I'm finally getting my priorities in order.''

15

◆◆◆◆◆

Camille dropped the three girls off at the mall early on Friday morning so that they could begin their Christmas shopping. Camille had also given Beth fifty dollars to spend. Terri immediately hooked up with LuAnne and Kasey and left Beth and Sloane to fend for themselves.

"Let's try this way." Beth pointed to the closest department store, in the opposite direction from where Terri had headed. In the juniors department, she searched through a dress rack.

"You looking for something in particular?"

"Just looking. How about you? Who's on your Christmas list?"

"I don't buy Christmas presents."

"Not for anyone?"

"Maybe my mom. I don't get my old man nothing. He's a creep."

"How about Carl?"

"Yeah. I'll get Carl something. Just not today."

Suddenly Beth realized that Sloane probably didn't have any money. "We could look for something, and then you could come back for it later."

"Carl don't want something from the stupid mall."

Beth was at a loss. Since she and Sloane had little in common, she was running out of ideas for entertaining her. At least Thanksgiving Day had gone well. Between the dinner and Camille's taking the girls to a movie so that Jack could watch football games on TV, the day had passed swiftly.

Sloane turned to her. "But don't let me keep you from your shopping. Who are you buying for?"

"My aunt and uncle, I guess. I'll have to mail Marcie and Teddy presents, so I should probably get something for them right away. They're my best friends back home."

Sloane looked uninterested. "How about Terri? You getting something for her? Not that she deserves it. She's not very nice to you."

"I guess I'll have to." She should have been shopping for gifts for her parents. For Allison. And for Doug. Tears filled her eyes.

"You all right?" Sloane took a step closer. "I bet you bought presents for your family every year, didn't you?"

Beth nodded, surprised at how Sloane had picked up on what was going through her mind.

"And now you got no family. Sort of like me."

"But you do!" Beth cried. "How can you say such a thing?"

Sloane snorted. "Just 'cause they're breathing air don't make them real parents. My brother, Nicky, left two years ago, and just as soon as I can, I'm leaving too. Let them kill each other."

Taking Sloane to the mall had been a mistake, Beth realized. Sloane didn't understand anything about traditions and family.

Sloane hated her family, and they were alive. Beth loved hers, and they were dead. It didn't make sense.

"Hey, do you want to do something that says 'in your face'?" Sloane asked. "Something that Terri and her little band of dweebs would never expect you to do?"

"Like what?"

"You want to get your belly button pierced?"

Beth recoiled. "Wouldn't it hurt?"

Sloane raised her T-shirt enough for Beth to see a small silver ring hanging from her navel. "No more than getting your ears done."

Beth stared in fascination at the silver ring. Neither her aunt nor her mother would have ever allowed her to do such a thing. Now there was no one to tell her what she could or couldn't do. This was a choice she could make by herself.

"Best part," Sloane continued, "is that nobody knows but you. As long as you keep it covered, of course. But once it's done, even if they find out, what're they going to do about it? It's your little secret."

My little secret. Terri and her crowd would

never do such a thing. Sloane was looking at Beth expectantly, and she realized that her answer would seal a sort of pact between them. They were from different worlds. Beth had always done what was expected of her; Sloane defied everybody. She was prickly and rude and . . . and *scared*. Despite all her bravado, Sloane Alonso was a scared little girl on the inside. Just like Beth.

"All right," Beth said. "I'll do it. But you've got to come with me."

Sloane's grin was quick and wicked. "Let's do it right now."

That night Sloane supervised Beth as she dabbed hydrogen peroxide on the pierced area. It hurt, but Beth felt immensely pleased every time she looked down and saw the small, glittery silver ring. All that evening she smiled with self-satisfaction, until Terri groused, "What are you so happy about?"

"Nothing."

"Well, you look dopey."

Sloane whistled casually, exasperating Terri so much that she shoved away from the table and marched out of the room.

"Now what's got into her?" Camille asked.

"Can't imagine," Beth said.

On Saturday night when the others had gone to bed, Beth and Sloane watched a movie on the VCR. Close to midnight, they heard a car horn give three short beeps. "That sounded like it came from our driveway." Beth went to the window.

Sloane bolted to the front door and flung it open. "It's Carl," she called over her shoulder. She signaled to him.

"What's he doing here? I thought you said he was out of town."

"He's back. I left a message on his friend's answering machine telling him where I was. He's here to get me."

"Now?" Beth couldn't believe it. "You can't leave now."

"Sure I can."

Carl approached the front door cautiously. "You ready?" he asked, giving Beth a nervous glance.

"Let me throw my stuff in my duffel bag." Sloane stood on tiptoes and kissed him.

"Missed you, babe."

"Is that your new car?" Sloane peered around him to the driveway.

"Nice, huh? It's got a lot under the hood. I averaged eighty all the way from Fort Payne."

Beth fidgeted. She didn't want her aunt and uncle to wake up, but how was she going to explain Sloane's slipping away in the night?

"Be right back." Sloane scooted down the hall, and Beth found herself alone with Carl. He was a big guy with muscular arms and a day's growth of beard.

"Thanks for letting her crash with you this weekend," he said.

"Um—no problem. We had a good time."

"I wouldn't have left if I'd known her old man was going to slap her around."

"I—I like her."

Carl grinned. "Yeah, she's pretty all right, to my way of thinking."

"You know, Fort Payne isn't too far from where I used to live in Chattanooga," Beth said to make conversation. "My dad took us to a concert there once."

Sloane came down the hall dragging her gear. "All set."

"I—I wish you wouldn't go," Beth stammered.

"Got to. Besides, I don't think Terri will miss me too much. Tell your aunt and uncle thanks. I had a good time."

Carl picked up Sloane's things, and Beth watched them hurry out to the car and drive off. She stood in the doorway staring down the empty street, feeling oddly bereft. Sloane's departure left silence and, for Beth, a void. While the two of them might never be the closest of friends, they had developed a connection that was important for each of them. When they'd needed someone, they'd found one another.

16

◆◆◆◆◆

"I heard you had a guest for Thanksgiving." Jared caught up with Beth in the hallway on Monday after their algebra test. "Everyone's talking about it."

She hugged her books to her chest. "All I did was take Sloane to my aunt's so she wouldn't have to camp out at school. What's to talk about?"

"Actually, you're sort of a hero."

She stopped short. "You're joking. Why is this such a big deal?"

"I'm not joking. Haven't you figured out by now that everybody at Westwood runs with their own kind? Cool kids with cool kids, nerds with nerds, losers with losers," he explained.

"So what am I?"

"That's the problem. They don't know where you fit. You start out with Terri the Stuck-up and move to Sloane the Unfavorable. In fact, you even take Sloane, the girl kids love to hate, into Terri's sacred territory. The way I hear it, Terri's really miffed. Mostly because you upstaged her, I think." A grin broke across his face. "Way to go, Beth."

She returned his smile. "My aunt and uncle were plenty mad when they found out she'd packed her stuff and taken off with Carl."

In truth, Camille had been horrified. She'd asked Beth, "Why didn't you stop her? Or at least, come get us so we could stop her?"

"It happened too fast," Beth had told them. "How was I supposed to keep her from leaving? Throw myself under Carl's wheels?"

Beth looked up at Jared. "Call me reckless. But I didn't do it to upset Terri. I did it to help out Sloane. You would have done the same thing."

"Probably, but kids expect it of me. Everybody knows I'm a rebel. You did it just because you're a nice person."

Beth felt her cheeks grow warm, and she knew she was blushing. "I—I like Sloane, you know."

Jared smiled. "And that's what makes you different, Beth. You look at people from the inside out instead of the other way around."

"That's a good thing?"

"That's a very good thing." Jared brushed her cheek, ever so softly, then left her standing in the hall with the feeling in her stomach of having swallowed a hundred butterflies.

Beth,

Got your present today and opened it without waiting till Christmas. The Orlando Magic shirt looks really cool. Thanks. The big news here—my brother is giving Shelby a ring for Christmas. Mom's not thrilled (they're too young, she says), but David's already bought it. It's sort of scary. David getting married and maybe having kids. Yikes! I'll be an uncle. I'm not ready for this.

Too bad you're not here. The church group is having a big party and going caroling. You know how bad I sing, but I'm going because Marcie's going. We both miss you, but I'm into your pretending game— I'm making believe you're just away for a week and will be back. I do that, you know—pretend you're coming back here to live.

Well, Mom's yelling at me to come with her to the mall, so I'll write more later. T.

P.S. My gift to you is in the mail.

Beth,

Our church youth group went Christmas caroling last night and I went with Teddy. Well, not exactly WITH him, but he went and I went, so that should count as a semi-date, don't you think? We went to the county old folks' home and walked the halls and sang happy Christmas songs. Except the home isn't a very happy place. Some of the patients were pretty out of it. One old woman grabbed my hand and asked, "Is that you, Tessie? Oh, Tessie, where have you been? Can you take me home?" I started to cry. Poor old lady! Anyway, Teddy put his arm around me and later when we were outside, he kissed me. Full on the mouth. I almost fainted.

Write soon. M. Your gift's in the mail—hope you like it!

Hey Marcie—
Sounds like you and Teddy are getting on pretty fine. That's good. You're both my friends. Still. No matter how much distance is between us.

This is the first year in my whole life ever that I'm dreading Christmas. I'm not kidding you, I wish I could go to sleep and wake up when it was all over. We decorated the tree on Saturday. Aunt Camille and Uncle Jack have an artificial tree, not a live one like we always had. Even after we got all the ornaments on, it still looked fake to me.

I'll never figure out Terri. One day she's nice to me, the next she hates me. She talks real rude to Aunt Camille sometimes too. But I bought her a Christmas present anyway. Did I tell you that Sloane gave me a pearl stud for my belly button? It's really cool. Course you're the only one besides her who knows I've had it pierced, and you're good at keeping secrets.

So here's another secret. I'll be glad when school's out next week. And glad when it starts up again. I feel all mixed up inside. And I wonder if my parents are looking down from heaven and seeing me. If they are, then they know how much I miss them. I wish Christmas would just go away this year. B.

"Why are you sitting alone in the dark, Aunt Camille?" Beth paused in the doorway of the living room. Camille sat on the sofa, staring at the Christmas tree.

"Thinking," Camille said. "Remembering."

Beth heard her aunt blow her nose and realized what she was thinking about.

"Would you come sit beside me?" Camille asked.

Hesitant, Beth walked to the sofa. "Do you want the lights on?"

"No."

The curtains were open, and the tree was silhouetted against the night sky. Without lights, the tree looked dreary and colorless. The presents had been opened that morning, and the floor beneath the tree now looked barren. A cold wave of loneliness spread through Beth, making her shiver.

"Did you have an okay Christmas?" her aunt asked.

"It was all right." Beth didn't want to tell her the truth—she'd had a horrible Christmas.

"No, it wasn't. Every one of us knew exactly what was missing."

Beth squeezed her hands into fists, letting her nails cut into her palms. She didn't want to burst out crying, and maybe the pain in her hands would substitute for the pain in her heart. "You and Uncle Jack gave me lots of presents. I—I really liked everything you got me."

"When I shopped this year, I saw so many things I wanted to get my sister." Camille's voice broke. "Every store had something. I'd hurry over and pick up it up and think to myself, 'Won't Carol love this!' and then I'd remember. Like a cold glass of water hitting me in the face—I'd remember. I'll never buy Carol a present again."

Camille reached over and wrapped her palm around Beth's closed fist. "Oh, Beth. I miss my sister so much. You're all I have of her. All that's left of her. Please, please don't ever leave me."

17

♦♦♦♦♦

"I—I don't know what you mean." Beth felt as if the air had been sucked from her. Camille's emotion was heavy, like a weight crushing Beth's chest.

"I know you're going to grow up and go away, Beth. You'll go to college. You'll get married. You'll move a thousand miles from us and I won't see you."

"But that'll be years from now."

"It doesn't matter. Without you, I don't have Carol." Camille leaned her head against the sofa cushion and stared up at the ceiling. "Sometimes when I hear your voice, you sound like Carol did when she was a kid.

And sometimes when I look at you, when the light hits you right, you look so much like your mother that I have to look twice just to make certain it isn't her."

"You think I look like Mom?"

"More than I ever looked like her. I took after Daddy's side of the family, but Carol was all Mom—your grandmother Talbert, that is."

"Mom used to talk to me about Grandma." Beth's mother's memories had been tender and interesting to a point. But sometimes Beth had grown bored with stories about a woman she had never—could never—meet.

Camille dabbed at her eyes. "Our mom died when you and Terri were barely a year old, and Carol and I missed her terribly. She was a wonderful mother."

You never get over losing your mother. The pain was with Camille to this day, Beth saw. Yet Camille's mother had died many years before. The same would hold true for Beth. The pain of her loss would never leave her, not completely anyway. The realization did not bring her comfort. She couldn't imagine going through the rest of her life with this terrible pain.

"Carol was so much like Mom," Camille said. "And you're so much like your mother. So all my memories get trotted out when I least expect it." She patted Beth's hand. "You understand what I'm saying, don't you?"

"I think so."

"And then add to it that I only had one child when I wanted several—well . . . it makes you all the more special to me, Beth."

"You're saying I'm like another daughter?" Hadn't Jack told her the same thing over Thanksgiving? Beth wondered how Terri would react to such a statement.

"Yes, you're another daughter to me. And you always will be." Camille blew her nose again and stuffed the tissue into the pocket of her robe. "I know I can't ever replace your mother in your heart, but I'll always be here for you."

"I know that," Beth said with a shrug. "And I know you and Uncle Jack are doing everything to make me feel at home." She didn't say, "But this isn't home," though that was what she was thinking.

"It's been five months since the accident."

"Five months, three weeks, and two days," Beth said. "To be exact."

"Getting through this isn't easy, Beth. It's going to take years."

Beth picked at a thread that had come loose on the arm of the sofa. It unraveled and she tugged, but it didn't come off. "Sometimes something happens and I think, 'Wait till I tell Mom.' Then I remember, there is no Mom to tell."

"You can tell me."

"It's not the telling," Beth explained. "It's the knowing I can't ever talk to her again. Or to Dad, or to Allison or Doug." She wrapped the thread around her finger and tugged hard. It stayed anchored.

"I know what you mean. Sometimes I think about all the things I wanted to say to them. The things I wanted to tell them. But I didn't, because I thought, 'I'll save it until next time I call,' or 'It'll keep until I see them next time.' Except there was no next time."

"I was crabby to Allison and Doug," Beth

said, her voice small and sad. "I should have been nicer."

"Don't think that way." Camille reached for Beth's free hand. "You were a good daughter. Your parents were so proud of you. Your mom bragged on you all the time. Every week when we talked she had some story to tell me about how terrific you were."

Slowly Beth unwrapped the thread from her finger. It wouldn't pull off. It would have to be cut. Just like her ties to her family. She patted the thread into place. Cutting it wasn't an option just now. "I'm glad you and Mom were close," she said. "It makes it easier knowing that you liked each other so much."

"We were close," Camille said. "That's what's making this Christmas extra difficult. They should be here."

"No, you should be up at our house," Beth said. "It was your turn to come visit us."

"So it was."

Beth cleared her throat. "What you said earlier, about me looking like Mom, well, sometimes when you laugh, I hear Mom.

Your laugh sounds a lot like hers. Sometimes when you're talking on the phone, I close my eyes and hear my mom.''

"Does it upset you?''

Beth thought about it. "No . . . it's a good thing. I don't want to forget.''

"A wise person once said that so long as one person remembers you, you'll never really be dead.''

"Maybe that's why you and Mom used to talk about Grandma Talbert so much—to keep her alive.''

Camille cocked her head and turned toward Beth. "Perhaps you're right. So that means anytime you want to talk about your mother, feel free to come to me.''

At the moment Beth couldn't imagine wanting to. Already this conversation had stirred up tremendous pain inside her heart. Her throat ached with the weight of unshed tears. And it was hard to keep pretending that her family was back home while she was just visiting her aunt and uncle. Talking about her family made the illusion fade, made the horror of her loss too real. Not trusting her voice, she nodded.

She stood. "I'm pretty tired.''

"Go on to your room," Camille urged. She caught Beth's hand. "Just remember this: We'll never have to get through the first Christmas without them again. We've done it. That milestone is behind us, and we'll never have to do it again."

Beth grasped her aunt's point, but it brought her little comfort. Certainly there would never be another first time, but there *would* be many more Christmases she'd have to spend without them. All the Christmases for the rest of her life.

"I saw you and Mom sitting in the living room in the dark." Terri's words sounded accusatory.

Beth was in her room, tinkering with her computer. Her cousin had come in unasked. "We were talking."

"I don't care." Terri jabbed Beth's shoulder, making her turn in the chair to face her. "But here's something you need to remember."

Terri's eyes were narrowed and looked glittering and hard. Beth looked up in genuine surprise. "And what's that?"

"She's *my* mother. And this is *my* house.

And you're just a relative. And even though everybody feels really sorry for you, you don't belong here.''

Terri spun on her heel and stalked from the room.

Stunned, unable to speak or move, Beth stared after her, feeling as if she'd just been struck hard across the face.

SPRING

18

"For a girl having a birthday party, you don't look very happy."

Jared's voice jarred Beth into the moment. She was at the ice-skating rink where her aunt and uncle were throwing her and Terri a joint birthday party. She had been sitting on a bench, staring moodily into the rink full of skaters, unwilling to join them. "I don't feel much like partying," she said as Jared sat down beside her.

"Didn't you tell me that once before?"

He was referring to the first time they met, when he'd found her half hiding beneath the banyan tree in LuAnne's yard. She smiled sheepishly. "Maybe so. But this is really Terri's party. I'm just baggage."

"The cake in the game room has your name on it too. I checked."

"You're the only one who showed up for me. When I asked Sloane, she said, 'No way.' She can't stand Terri and said she wouldn't fit in. She was sorry, but . . ." Beth shrugged. "I don't hold it against her or anything. I understand how she feels."

"You could have invited others."

"There was no one else I wanted to invite."

"So you have a fifty percent turnout. What's so bad about that?"

She looked at him and felt self-conscious, ashamed. "I didn't mean it the way it sounded. I'm really glad you showed up. It was nice of you."

"Hey, there was free cake." He grinned.

"I don't feel fifteen," Beth said, hanging her head and scuffing her shoes against the wooden floor.

"How's fifteen supposed to feel?"

"Happy."

He stood and hauled her up beside him.

"Come outside with me for a minute. It's too noisy in here."

They went out into the parking lot, where the March air felt warm. She slipped off her sweater and tied it around her waist. Stars glittered in the dark sky, and light from an overhead lamp cast a circle of yellow on the asphalt where they stood. "I can't get used to the weather here," she said. "Back home, it's usually still cold on my birthday."

"I've heard about spring," Jared said. "Never experienced it myself, though."

"I'm sorry I'm acting so dopey. I know I'm no fun to be around."

"Maybe this will cheer you up." He held out a small box.

"For me?" For some reason it surprised her. Then she reminded herself that it *was* her birthday, after all.

"No, for Terri."

She smiled up at him, then shook the box. "Is it a pony?"

"Man, I can't ever fool you."

She ripped off the paper and discovered a small, intricately carved wooden jewelry box.

"I heard you had a collection of belly button rings," he said.

She blushed because he knew such an intimate thing about her. "Sloane told you? Can't I have any secrets?"

"Don't be mad. I sweated it out of her."

She smiled again to show she'd been teasing. "Thanks. Really. I like it a lot."

"It came from India. At least that's what the lady at the store told me." He put his hands on her shoulders. "One other thing," he said.

She looked up expectantly.

"Happy birthday, Beth." Without warning, he lifted her chin and kissed her full on the lips. The kiss was quick; she didn't even have time to close her eyes.

Her breath caught, her heart thudded, and the world seemed to tilt. She drew back. His face was shielded from the light, so she couldn't see his expression. She fought against touching her fingertips to her mouth, where she could still feel the slight pressure of his lips. She didn't know what to say. No boy had ever kissed her before, not in the way Jared just had. "I—I—"

"Better get back," he said, cutting off

words she didn't have anyway. He put his arm around her and walked her inside.

Sloane was crying. Her nose had turned red, and her mascara made black rings under her eyes. They were outside school the day before spring break was to begin. Feeling helpless, Beth asked, "But are you absolutely sure you won't pass?"

"Mr. Holwerda told me so," Sloane said, wiping her nose on her sleeve. "He said I missed too many days so I'll have to repeat."

Beth fumbled in her purse for a tissue. If the principal had told Sloane she was going to fail, it must be true. "Why'd you miss so much?"

"I skipped." Sloane took the tissue and gave Beth a sullen look. "School's boring. It's more fun doing other things."

"Then why are you so broken up about it?"

"Because I'll be left behind while everybody else goes on to high school. I don't want to be left behind." She shook her head. "Boy, my old man's going to be pissed."

"What will he do to you?" Beth's heart seemed to contract at the prospects.

"Yell and scream and call me stupid. That's what he always does."

"Can't you go to summer school?"

"I won't go to summer school. It sucks." Carl drove up. The noise from his faulty muffler drowned out Sloane's voice. She jumped up from the stone bench where she was sitting with Beth and grabbed her stuff.

Beth took Sloane's arm. "Would you like to talk some more about it? Maybe spend the weekend with me?"

"I'm through talking." Sloane freed her arm and rushed over to the car. She tossed her books through the open window and jerked open the door.

Feeling helpless, Beth watched Carl drive away.

"Something has come up."

Those were the first words out of her aunt's mouth when Beth arrived home from school.

"Like what?"

"The realtor called to say that the renters are moving."

"So find more renters."

"There's more." Camille took a deep

breath. "The bank that holds the mortgage wrote to inform us that the house must be sold in order to settle your parents' estate."

Beth heaved her books onto the kitchen counter. "That's *my* family's house. The bank can't just sell it without permission."

"Yes, they can. Technically, the bank owns the house. Just remember, though, once the house is sold and the mortgage is paid, the remainder will go into your trust fund—"

"I don't care! It's my house. You can't let them sell it, Aunt Camille."

Camille tried to put her arm around Beth, but Beth stepped away. "Beth, I can't stop it. Jack's talked to the bank and to your parents' attorney. It's the only way. Our hands are tied. I'm sorry, honey."

"It isn't *fair.*"

"None of it's been fair, Beth. I wish I could change things, but I can't."

In her mind's eye, Beth envisioned the house she'd grown up in. The halls where Allison had drawn on the walls with crayons when she'd been five. The stained carpet on the stairs where Doug had spilled grape juice. She saw the house as it had once been—her room, her parents' room, the family room, the huge credenza along the wall that had been one of her mother's antique finds. Some bank was taking even more of her past away. "I know it's not your fault, Aunt Camille. I know you tried."

Camille's face was full of sympathy. "Try not to dwell on it, Beth. It's only a house. We've got the important things out of it already."

Beth felt numb, as if all the blood had been drained out of her. It was happening to her again—impersonal, faceless, unfeeling, uncaring forces she could not see, could not fight were manipulating her life once more. And, just as always, there was absolutely *nothing* she could do about it. She left the kitchen without another word.

19

◆◆◆◆◆

Jared took Beth to a movie at the mall on Friday night, and when it was over, they hooked up with Sloane and Carl at the food court.

The minute Beth sat down, Sloane leaned over and said, "You still broken up about your parents' house being sold? I told Carl how hard it hit you."

Carl uttered a swear word to reinforce Sloane's statement.

Beth toyed with the straw in her soda and said, "I know I should be handling it better. I'm being such a baby about it. But I can't stop thinking about the house. I want to see it so bad.''

''Wouldn't your aunt take you to see it if you asked her?'' Jared asked.

''She hasn't got the time now. And it'll probably be sold by summer when she does. No. . . . I'll never see my home again.''

''You really want to see it again? Is it that important to you?'' Carl's voice, deep and deliberate, sliced through the noise from the surrounding tables.

Beth said, ''More than anything.''

''Then let's go.'' He sounded matter-of-fact.

''Now? Right now? Are you kidding?''

''Why not?'' He put his arm around Sloane. ''Me and Sloane will take you. If we leave tonight, we can be in Chattanooga by tomorrow morning.''

''Sure,'' Sloane said, looking eager. ''We could drive all night. It'll be fun. An adventure.''

Beth's heart began to thud as the magnitude of Carl's offer sank in. ''You really mean it?''

''Can you spot me some dough for gas?''

"Sure." She sat up straighter, every nerve in her body tingling.

"What about your aunt and uncle?" Jared asked. "Won't they notice if you don't come home?"

"They're away until Sunday. They've gone to some weekend marriage seminar. They're staying at a hotel downtown, and left Terri and me on our good behavior."

"Won't Terri call and tell them if you take off?"

Sloane gave a disgusted snort. "I won't be around to shut her up, you know."

Beth felt let down. Could Terri be trusted to keep her mouth shut through the weekend? "I don't know. Let's go ask her."

They stood. Jared took her hand. "Are you sure about this, Beth?"

Carl's offer had carried her from the pit of despair to the height of hope in a matter of moments. Taking off was bold, even scary, but the more she thought about it, the more it made sense. It wasn't as if she were running away, she told herself. She was simply going home—to the place where she belonged. "Yes," she told Jared. "I'm positive."

Jared walked with her out to Carl's car. "I'd go with you if I could." He closed the car door once she was inside. "Remember who your friends are. I'll be here when you come back, all right?"

He assumed she would be returning. For a brief moment she felt torn. Jared was special. She cared about him, and he'd shown her that he cared for her. But she was so mixed up inside right then, she couldn't think straight. Her present was all around her and she saw that it was good, but her past was calling to her. "I'll be in touch," she told him, keeping it vague because she didn't know what was going to happen to her. She simply didn't know.

"Are you crazy? You can't just run off!" Terri flailed her arms and followed Beth around her room while she packed things in a duffel bag.

"And why can't I?" Beth turned to face her cousin. "You've never wanted me here anyway. What do you care if I leave?"

"That's not fair. I've tried to be nice to you."

Beth snorted. "When? Last Christmas,

when you told me this was *your* house and Aunt Camille was *your* mother and I'd better not forget it?"

Terri's face flushed. "I—I was mad. When I saw the two of you talking and crying together, I felt left out. Ever since you came here, Mom and Dad have talked about nothing but poor Beth, and how to make Beth happy, and how I needed to share my school and my friends and my life—"

"You were jealous?" Beth couldn't believe her ears. "You want to change places with me, Terri? You want to have your parents die, and come live with me, and leave your friends and everything behind?"

Tears swam in Terri's eyes. In a small voice she squeaked, "No."

"I didn't think so." Beth returned to her packing. "Sloane and Carl are waiting. I've got to hurry. Would you please move out of my way?"

Terri stepped aside. "But Mom and Dad . . . what will I tell them?"

"Don't tell them anything until Sunday night when they come home. Can you do that much for me?"

"They'll kill me."

"Probably not."

"They'll come and get you, you know."

"Maybe you can talk them out of it. Especially since you don't want me around."

Terri started crying. "That's not true. I want you to stay. I—I've gotten used to having you here. Sort of like a sister."

Beth looked at her sobbing cousin and for a moment felt sorry for her. "I had a sister. Believe me, you've never treated me like one."

"Oh, sure . . . like you were never rude to Allison. I heard you chew her out more than once."

Guilt stabbed at Beth. Terri was right— she hadn't always treated Allison well. Why, she even used to fuss at her sister for something as dumb as using her shampoo. "That's true. I wasn't very nice to her sometimes. But that never meant I didn't care."

"Well, I care about you, too," Terri said stubbornly.

Beth zipped her bag and heaved it off the bed. "Then keep my secret for a couple of days. I lived most of my life on Signal Mountain. And I have Marcie and Teddy there too, so it's not like I'll be in the streets. I'll be fine." She threw out the last part just to needle Terri. To let her know she thought Terri selfish and uncaring.

Beth was almost across her room and to the door when Terri blurted out, "They were getting a divorce. Mom and Dad . . . they were calling it quits."

Beth stopped in her tracks and spun around. Terri had clamped her hand across her mouth, but her eyes were wide and her face looked as if it were about to crumble.

"*Your* parents?" Beth said. "*My* aunt and uncle?"

Terri nodded, tears running freely down her cheeks. "They didn't think I knew, but I heard them talking about it—I knew, all right. Then the accident happened. And you came and they stopped talking about it. They wouldn't have stayed together for me, but they would for you."

Beth felt hot and cold at the same time. Had her mom and dad known about Jack and Camille? She thought back to when Jack had told her he was reexamining his priorities. And to when Camille had said to her that the time to tell someone something important was when the person was alive and you *could* tell them. "I—I'm sure they changed their minds because they wanted to keep your family together," Beth said, still reeling from Terri's revelation. "Family's important. It was the *most* important thing to my parents, I think."

"Well, it wasn't to mine." Terri swiped at her damp cheeks and squared her shoulders. "I won't call them, Beth. I won't tell them until Sunday. Promise."

Beth said thank you, got partway through the door, then hurried back and gave Terri a quick, fierce hug. She bolted down the stairs and out to the car, where Sloane and Carl waited. Slamming the car door, she said, "Let's go."

Carl pulled out of the driveway and headed for the expressway, glancing once in his rearview mirror at Beth hunched in the corner of the backseat. "You two better get some sleep," he said. "It's going to be a long night."

20

◆◆◆◆◆

With Beth directing him, Carl drove down the quiet streets of her old neighborhood. They had stopped only to have breakfast at a Waffle House outside Atlanta. The long trip faded as she stared out the window at the neighborhood where she'd grown up, at the rows of Victorian-style houses surrounded by green, clipped lawns and tall, stately trees. At the end of a cul-de-sac, Beth said, "Here. Stop here."

The house, *her* house, looked in need of a paint job. A shutter on one of the upstairs windows hung loose. True to her word, though, Faye Carpenter had kept up the flowerbeds. Tulips and purple iris bloomed between neat rows of colorful pansies. Soon it would be time to plant begonias, impatiens, and geraniums, just as Beth's mother had planted them every year.

Carl parked in the driveway, and Beth got out. Her legs were stiff from sitting, but the air felt cool and smelled clean, like freshly washed laundry. On the porch she saw the realtor's lock box hanging on the front door handle. "It's locked," she said in dismay.

"I'll get you in," Carl said. He removed a crowbar from the trunk of his car and jimmied a window behind the front porch.

"What if someone calls the cops?" Sloane asked.

"It's *my* house," Beth said. "I can be here if I want."

When the window was open, Carl asked, "You want us to go in with you?"

"No. Please . . . this is something I want to do by myself."

He shrugged and sat down with Sloane on the porch steps. Beth squeezed through the window. She shivered; the house was cold. No heat had come through the furnace vents in weeks. And, of course, it was empty. All the furniture she'd grown up with was still in storage, and the renters had taken theirs with them.

Beth walked toward the kitchen, her shoes making a hollow sound on the floor. The kitchen smelled musty; the walls looked grungy. She returned to the foyer, to the stairs, and climbed them. Ghosts trailed after her . . . ghosts and memories. She saw marks on the wall behind the bathroom door where her father had measured her, Allison, and Doug as they'd grown. She heard her mother say, "They make special charts for the backs of doors, Paul. Can't we buy one and save the walls?"

And she heard her father reply, "It's a tradition, Carol. Everyone makes marks on their walls for this sort of thing. You don't want the kids to grow up without traditions, do you?"

Beth stepped into her bedroom. The tenants had put up wallpaper for a nursery. Bright balloons and circus clowns made the room look strange. Not like Beth's room at all. Sunlight was pouring through the window and spilling onto the carpet around her feet. Beyond lay a sea of shadows. The golden glow of her childhood was gone. She couldn't bring it back.

She wandered down the hall, stopped, and swung open the door to her parents' bedroom. She half expected to see their king-sized bed, but all that remained of it was a faint outline on the wallpaper. She eased herself down to the carpet and clutched her knees against her chest.

Gone! They were all gone. The house was a shell, left behind by life. Tears stung her eyes.

She heard a commotion coming from downstairs and jumped to her feet. She ran down the hall, rushed down the stairs, and saw Carl blocking Teddy from coming inside. "It's all right," she yelled.

"Beth? Is that you?"

She didn't answer. She flung herself into Teddy's arms and burst into soul-wrenching sobs.

"I can't believe this. You're here. You're actually here!" Beth was sitting in Teddy's kitchen, and Faye was pouring them a round of hot chocolate and talking a mile a minute. "I still think we should call your aunt's. If even just to let your cousin know you got here safely."

"Don't worry. Aunt Camille will be calling us Sunday." Beth had explained how her impromptu trip had come about. Now that she was home, she didn't want to think about Tampa.

"We've got to split." Carl had gulped his chocolate and was standing, impatient to leave.

"Where will you go?" Faye asked.

"Fort Payne's only an hour away, and that's where my uncle lives. I'm taking Sloane to meet him."

Beth walked out with Sloane and Carl. "I really appreciate your bringing me."

"Glad we could do it," Carl said.

Beth turned to Sloane. "Guess I'll see you . . . whenever."

"Maybe not," Sloane said. "Me and Carl may just stay in Alabama. Nothing much for me back home, you know."

Beth didn't know what to say. Change was happening all around her. She was home, but everything was different. She had ties back in Tampa, but she didn't know what to do about them. She felt suspended between two worlds, like a fly stuck to a screen, looking into one place, unable to leave the other behind. "You take care of yourself," she told Sloane.

"Don't I always?" Sloane grinned.

Beth waved goodbye.

"We've missed you," Faye said when Beth returned to the kitchen.

"And I've missed everybody here."

"Teddy shared your e-mail with us. A good thing. It made it easier."

"You did a nice job on the flowerbeds. They really look pretty—just like Mom would have kept them."

Faye waved away Beth's compliment. "Your mother was my best friend. I loved doing it for her. I miss her very much. I've missed your whole family. I miss watching you grow up, Beth. These have been the saddest months of my life."

Teddy hauled himself up from the table. "So why don't I take Beth around to see everybody? That's why she came." Once they were outside, he added, "Thought we should blow the place. I was afraid Mom would start bawling in front of you."

"I've cried plenty, that's for sure."

They walked around to the side of the house, where they'd spent so many hours playing Horse over the years. "You know Marcie's out of town, don't you?" he said.

"She told me she was going to her grandmother's in Kentucky. If I'd planned this trip, I'd have made sure I came when she was here, but it wasn't planned. You know I want to see her." She pursed her lips. "You still kissing her?"

Teddy turned a deep shade of red. "Who told you that?"

"Who do you think? We're friends, you know."

"You still kissing that guy down in Tampa? What's his name?"

Beth gasped. "Marcie! That little rat fink. I told her not to tell."

Teddy grinned. "We used to be friends and you told me everything."

"Not that." Beth's cheeks grew warm. Partly because Jared's face and smile and the way he'd looked at her the night he'd kissed her jumped into her memory. She half expected him to materialize so that she could introduce him to Teddy. "You'd like Jared. He reminds me of you in some ways."

Teddy picked up the basketball. "Want to shoot a few?"

"I'm rusty."

"Can't kick my butt anymore?"

She snatched the ball. "Let me warm up." She dribbled and shot. And missed.

"It's good to have you home again, Beth. If there's anything you want to do, tell me."

She said, "I want to go to the cemetery. I want to be with my family again."

21

◆◆◆◆◆

It rained. For three days a hard, drenching rain kept Beth captive at Teddy's house. Flash flood warnings and downed trees and power lines held the city at a standstill. By the time the skies cleared and the sun shone again, Camille and Terri had arrived from Florida.

Camille was hardly out of her car and reacquainted with Faye before she hauled Beth into the Carpenters' spare bedroom, where Beth was staying. There she confronted Beth, demanding, "What were you thinking? How could you run off this way?

Don't you know how worried Jack and I have been?''

Beth was prepared for her aunt's anger. "I never meant to upset you. I just wanted to see my house before it was sold," she explained calmly.

"I would have brought you. All you had to do was ask."

"The chance to come came up real sudden, so I took it."

"Well, you should have used better judgment. Terri too. She should have called immediately and told us what was going on."

Terri had kept her promise to Beth, and for that Beth was grateful. She didn't want her cousin to get into any more hot water than she was in already. "Don't be mad at Terri. I made her promise to wait until you came home from your weekend. Was the seminar all right?''

"Yes, it was worthwhile, and I'm glad we went," Camille said. "But that doesn't excuse what you did. Our going away for the weekend was no license for you to run off."

"I wasn't running away. I just wanted to come home, and I knew Teddy's folks would let me stay with them. I've been perfectly safe, you know."

"I know that," Camille said. "It's just that you had no right to take off that way."

"If I'd asked permission to go with Sloane and Carl, would you have let me come?"

Camille's face reddened. "That's not the point."

"You wouldn't have." Answering her own question, Beth shook her head for emphasis. "I wanted to come home, Aunt Camille. Is that so hard to understand?"

"But your home is with us now. I don't want to lose you too, Beth." Camille sighed. "Did coming here, seeing the house, make it better for you?"

Torn, Beth hugged her arms to herself. "When I went through the house, I thought I'd be close to my family again, but I wasn't. It was freaky to see the rooms and remember where all the furniture had been. I could still hear Mom's and Dad's voices. I could still see Allison and Doug running down the halls. Except, not really. It was only make-believe. The renters had changed some things. I know they had every right to, but I felt like they were intruders, like they didn't belong in our space."

"Beth—I'm so sorry about the house. Really, if there was anything I could do—"

Beth shook her head. "No, it's okay. The house isn't really important to me. Not anymore. I came to see it, and I did. But I know I don't belong there. Not without them."

Camille's eyes glistened with tears. "We'll stay a few days, I promise. We'll let you visit with your friends. We'll do anything you want to do. No rush."

"There's school." Beth remembered that school would be starting up the first of the week, and she had a paper due in English and a big test in algebra. And she wondered how Jared was doing, and if he missed her.

"You and Terri both can take a few days off from school. It's no big deal. This is more important."

"Thank you," Beth said. But the victory felt hollow because it wasn't really about staying or leaving her old house and old friends and old city. It was about saying goodbye to herself in this place. It was about finding a new Beth inside the old one.

* * *

Teddy had gone off to his part-time job at McDonald's, Camille was in the kitchen with Faye, and Beth was shooting baskets when Terri came outside that evening.

"You're pretty good," Terri said.

"I'm pretty rusty," Beth said, watching the ball sail through the bent hoop.

"You should go out for basketball next year. Bet you'd be on the team in a flash. I'm not very good at sports myself."

Beth caught the ball and held it. Turning to Terri, she said, "Thanks for keeping quiet about me going off. That couple of days' head start was a good thing. I know you got into trouble because you covered for me, and I appreciate it."

Terri shrugged. "Mom and Dad got over it once they realized you were all right. They've just grounded me for a few weeks."

"I'm sorry about that."

"I was pretty scared that first night all alone by myself. I locked all the doors and stuck a baseball bat under the covers with me. I'll bet I didn't sleep half an hour."

This information surprised Beth. She

hadn't even considered that her going when she did would leave Terri feeling frightened. "I'm sorry—"

"It's okay. No boogeyman came to get me." Terri smiled shyly. "And on Saturday I had the whole place to myself. I raided the fridge, watched TV till my eyes crossed, talked on the phone whenever I felt like it. But I didn't tell a soul I was by myself." Terri looked proud of that. "I—I didn't realize how much your being down the hall had come to mean to me until you weren't there."

"I thought you hated me living there."

Terri poked at the ground with the toe of her sneaker. "Some days I did. At first I felt really sorry for you. And I thought I was going to be your best friend. I thought I'd introduce you around to all my friends and we'd all hang out together. I thought . . . well, a lot of things. But you didn't like my friends. You didn't want to be around them. Or me."

Beth felt her cheeks grow warm. Everything Terri was saying was true.

"It's all right," Terri added hastily. "It's just that things didn't go the way I expected. And Mom and Dad kept bending over backward to make sure you were happy. And you kept ignoring me. You made friends with Sloane, the toughest girl in the school. A girl who hated me. And then Jared liked you and not me."

"I—I didn't mean to—"

"That's okay too." Terri's eyes were diamond bright with tears. "I know I'll never win the Miss Popularity contest at Westwood. Thinking I could get Jared to like me was dumb from the start. But of everything that happened, the very worst part is that nobody seemed to care that I lost Aunt Carol and Uncle Paul just like everyone else did. And you and Allison and Doug are the only cousins I'll ever have. My family's never been close like yours, you know. You did everything together. Dad worked all the time, and Mom and I usually argue and fight." She shrugged. "I'm not sure why."

Beth had never honestly seen the situation through Terri's eyes. She'd never once considered the impact of her tragedy on Terri's life. All at once, Terri's brattiness and hostility made more sense. "Well, you're right—I didn't think much about anything, or anybody, for a long time."

"I thought you hated me," Terri said. "And I didn't know how to fix myself so that you'd like me."

"It irked me that you had a mother you didn't treat very nicely, while I had no mother at all," Beth confessed. "I know we're related, but I didn't feel close to you."

A wry smile crossed Terri's mouth. "Well, you know what they say: 'You can pick your friends, but you can't pick your relatives.'"

Emotion clogged Beth's throat as she heard her mother's words from Terri. "My mom used to tell me that."

"Yeah, me too. When I asked her why you didn't like me, that's what she'd say."

"You talked to my mom about us?"

"Aunt Carol was the best listener in the whole world. I talked to her every chance I got."

More information Beth had never heard.

Twilight had gathered, and Faye called out to them to come in for ice-cream sundaes. Beth put the ball down. "Guess we'd better go in."

Terri started after her. Beth stopped and caught her cousin's arm. "Will you promise me something?"

"What?"

"Be nicer to your mother, Terri. Not so snippy. I'm not being bossy, just letting you know you sound mean when you talk to her sometimes. That makes me crazy."

Terri nodded. "And will you promise that you'll stop ignoring me? That you'll stop treating me like I'm a nobody, and like the things I like are stupid and childish?"

Beth studied her cousin's face. Her eyes were brown, like Uncle Jack's, but she had her mother's high cheekbones. It was a trait Beth had shared with her mother too—high cheekbones and deep-set eyes. In the pale purple light, she saw the faintest traces of her mother's smile on her cousin's face. The recognition was startling, yet oddly comforting. "All right," Beth told Terri, trembling. "We'll make a pact about it. We'll both try harder to think of the other's feelings."

"Fair enough," Terri said.

"Fair enough," Beth echoed.

22

◆◆◆◆◆

The next morning Beth got her wish and returned to the cemetery. Aunt Camille drove, and Terri came along.

She made her way between the long aisles of neatly manicured grass as the sun warmed her shoulders. In the distance a caretaker trimmed hedges, while another planted rows of impatiens along a footpath. She walked quickly, her heart tight in her chest, reading the small metal plaques as she passed among those buried.

PAUL HAXTON. She stopped. She'd almost missed it. On the day of the funeral, there had been a canopy, a crowd, a hole in the ground, covered by a tarpaulin. But the grass had done its work; now the ground looked lush and green. No scars remained, no telltale signs of that terrible day last summer.

Beth sank to her knees. Beside her father's marker, her mother's rested. CAROL TALBERT HAXTON. Next to hers were Allison's and Doug's. In a neat little row they lay. Side by side. Together beneath the ground. She struggled to see their faces as they had been that last morning. The images weren't there! Why? It had been so easy for so many months to recapture their faces. But suddenly it was as if there were a rip in her memory and all the pictures had leaked out. Panic filled Beth. Why couldn't she see their faces?

She heard Terri and her aunt come up and stoop down beside her. She didn't want them to suspect that her memory had failed. They'd think she was callous, uncaring. "I should have gone with them that day," she said. "I should have."

"Then you would be dead too," Camille said. "And we would have *none* of you with us."

"I should have made them stay home

with me. Mom said she would, but I told her no. I watched them drive away. I could have stopped them.''

"We can't keep the people we love safe, no matter how hard we try.''

Terri patted the grass over her aunt's grave. "I miss you, Aunt Carol.''

In a rush the images of Beth's family returned, tumbling through her mind like scattered leaves. With great relief, Beth sat back on her haunches. "I don't want to forget them.''

"You won't,'' Camille assured her. "Their memory will grow dimmer, but it's a light that will never go out.''

Death had forgotten Beth. It had left her behind. She had been spared. For what? "Why?'' she asked. "Why them and not me?''

"I think that's what life's journey is all about. Discovering the whys, the reasons we've been put here on earth. Some people never know. The lucky ones find work to do that makes them whole and gives them value.''

Beth wanted things to be normal again.

She wanted to go home and find her mother fixing lunch and Allison and Doug watching TV. She wanted to see her father mowing the lawn. "Do you think they can see us? Up in heaven, when they look down. Can they see us?"

"I'm sure of it," Camille said.

"Allison and Doug never got to grow up." Beth wondered if angels would kiss them.

"True," Camille said. "But how many children get to walk into heaven holding their mother's and father's hands?"

"Not many," Beth admitted. The image comforted her. Still, she saw the vacant spot where she should have been. "Will they remember me? When I get to heaven? Will they know who I am?"

Camille traced her sister's name on the brass plate with the tip of her finger. "When you die an old woman and walk up to heaven's gate, Allison and Doug will run to meet you. They'll take your hand and show you off to everyone."

Beth was separated from her family. For a while. For the span of her lifetime. She would go on, and when her time was over, she would be with them. In the meantime, it was up to her to spin the straw of her life into gold.

She looked at her aunt, and then at her cousin. She and Terri would grow up together. Side by side. They would adjust, compromise, change, accept. They would learn to get along—just like sisters. Beth took Terri's hand and then Aunt Camille's. They were family. She had no other. And they wanted her. "I'm ready to go home," she said.

Together they walked out of the cemetery. And this time it was Beth who left death behind.

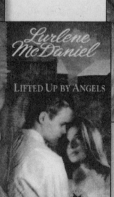

DO WISHES COME TRUE WHEN YOU WISH UPON A STAR?

ISBN: 0-553-57130-3

You won't want to miss Lurlene McDaniel's special hardcover edition featuring three heartwarming and inspirational novellas that capture the true spirit of the holiday season.